Shattered love . . .

"If anyone here knows of any reason why these two should not be joined in matrimony, let him speak now, or forever—"

"Stop!" Danny shouted, jumping to his feet.

The wedding guests reacted to Danny's outburst as if a gun had been fired. People jumped to their feet, shouting questions at Danny.

"Why on earth shouldn't this couple be married?" Captain Avedon demanded.

"Because the bride has been two-timing the groom," Danny shouted.

Now that Danny had said the words, there was no turning back. He wished the floor would swallow him up. Instead, several of the people he loved most in the world were staring at him as if he were a monster.

Bantam Books in the Sweet Valley University series
Ask your bookseller for the books you have missed

And don't miss these
Sweet Valley University Thriller Editions:

SWEET VALLEY UNIVERSITY™

Shipboard Wedding

Written by
Laurie John

Created by
FRANCINE PASCAL

BANTAM BOOKS
NEW YORK · TORONTO · LONDON · SYDNEY · AUCKLAND

RL 6, age 12 and up

SHIPBOARD WEDDING

A Bantam Book / August 1995

Sweet Valley High® and Sweet Valley University™
are trademarks of Francine Pascal
Conceived by Francine Pascal
Produced by Daniel Weiss Associates, Inc.
33 West 17th Street
New York, NY 10011

ISBN: 0-553-56693-8

Published simultaneously in the United States and Canada

Bantam Books are published by Bantam Books, a division of Bantam
Doubleday Dell Publishing Group, Inc. Its trademark, consisting of the
words "Bantam Books" and the portrayal of a rooster, is Registered in
U.S. Patent and Trademark Office and in other countries. Marca
Registrada. Bantam Books, 1540 Broadway, New York, New York 10036.

PRINTED IN THE UNITED STATES OF AMERICA

OPM   0 9 8 7 6 5 4 3 2 1

To Alice Elizabeth Wenk

Chapter One

"Jessica! Jessica, are you in there?" Elizabeth Wakefield knocked on the door of the cabin she and her twin sister, Jessica, shared and listened intently for Jessica's answering shout. "Jessica?" she repeated, stepping inside.

Silence.

Elizabeth hurried to the bathroom and banged on the door. When there was no answer, she walked in. Maybe Jessica had slipped and hit her head on the counter or fainted in the shower . . .

But no body lay prone on the bathroom floor—or anyplace else. Jessica wasn't in the cabin. She wasn't in the dining room. She wasn't in any of the shops. She wasn't on any of the decks.

She'd disappeared.

Elizabeth left the cabin and shut the door, her heart thumping uncomfortably in her chest. Jessica had already fallen overboard once. Was it

1

possible that she had slipped and fallen again?

It seemed unlikely that anything that disastrous could happen twice. On the other hand, very few things were "unlikely" when it came to her twin. With Jessica, a disaster could happen not only twice, but twice a day.

On the outside, Jessica and Elizabeth were identical. Both girls were tall and slim, with golden skin and blue-green eyes the color of the sea. And both girls had the long, straight golden blond hair that was the hallmark of the true California girl.

But inside, the girls were as different as night and day. Elizabeth had always been studious, down to earth, and fiercely protective of Jessica.

Jessica was impulsive, romantic, and emotional. And she seemed to have a genius for getting herself—and Elizabeth—into difficult and sometimes dire straits.

Suddenly Elizabeth was sick with fear. It wasn't like Jessica to vanish for so long. Especially when she didn't have a boyfriend to steal away with.

Elizabeth ran across the deck nearest their cabin and peered over the rail at the dark water. "Jessica!" she cried, knowing as she called out that it was futile. Even if Jessica were somewhere in the water, she would never hear Elizabeth's voice over the roar of the SS *Homecoming Queen*'s engines. "Jessica!" she screamed again. Now her voice reflected all the panic and fear she had been keeping in check.

A gentle hand closed around her upper arm. "Elizabeth. What's the matter?"

With tears running down her cheeks, Elizabeth turned to face Isabella Ricci, one of Jessica's best friends.

"It's Jessica," Elizabeth said. "I can't find her anywhere."

Isabella's frown relaxed. "And you think she went overboard? Don't be silly. Not even Jessica could manage to fall overboard twice on one cruise."

"I know it seems ridiculous," Elizabeth said, wiping her tears away with the back of one hand. "But this whole cruise seems to be so ill fated, I just keep waiting for the next disaster. Nothing would surprise me at this point."

Isabella's beautiful face broke into a sympathetic smile, and she brushed her long curtain of dark hair back off her shoulders. "You're exaggerating. There've just been a few . . . well . . . misadventures."

"*Catastrophes,*" Elizabeth insisted tearfully. "And we haven't had a *few* of them. We've had a lot of them. I planned this cruise thinking it would give everybody a chance to recover from the William White nightmare. It was supposed to be the greatest spring break any of us had ever had. Instead . . ." Elizabeth's voice trailed off as she contemplated the numerous things that had gone wrong since the ship had set sail.

3

Bryan Nelson had been having such a miserable time, he left after the first day. Now his girlfriend, Nina Harper, had no idea where he was. She was trying to act as if she didn't care by dating the ship's doctor, but Elizabeth knew how much Nina cared about Bryan—and only Bryan.

Winston Egbert and Denise Waters had been left behind on some island, and no one knew when and if they'd turn up again.

Leonardo di Mondicci, the brother of Lila Fowler's late husband, had shown up and caused trouble between her and Bruce Patman—now both of them were miserable. And when Leonardo wasn't busy guilt-tripping Lila, he was romancing Alexandra Rollins. And that was making Alex's boyfriend, Noah Pearson, totally gloomy and down in the dumps.

Jessica had fallen overboard and nearly drowned. Elizabeth's mind whirled with the enormity of what had gone wrong. She willed herself not to think about the most painful event of all, but her mind conjured up the image of her boyfriend, Tom Watts, unbidden. "And Tom . . ." Elizabeth's lip trembled. "And Tom . . ."

"I know," Isabella said softly.

Elizabeth didn't finish. She couldn't. Seeing Tom in the arms of Nicole Riley had been the coup de grâce. He had tried to apologize, but how could Elizabeth ever trust him again?

"First of all," Isabella said in her usual calm and

4

reasonable tone, "it's not your fault Bryan left. It was his own fault. He and Nina were having some problems, and rather than trying to work them out, he acted like a sulky kid. So Nina did what any self-respecting independent woman would do—she made up her mind to have fun with or without him. Stop blaming yourself. That's between Nina and Bryan."

Elizabeth nodded. Isabella was right. But she still couldn't help feeling awful. Nina was her best friend. "I thought I was giving her a great gift when I bought the tickets for the cruise. But all I did was break up her relationship with Bryan."

Isabella took Elizabeth's arm and shook it. "Quit trying to make yourself responsible for everybody and everything. If anybody owes anybody an apology, it's Bryan. He never should have left. And Nina is having a great time, as far as I can see. Dr. Daniels seems like he's crazy about her, and they look like they're having a blast together. As for Winston and Denise . . ." Isabella tapped her foot nervously on the deck. "Getting left behind was their own fault too. Both of them knew when the ship was leaving. And both of them know how to tell time."

"Do you think they'll catch up?" Elizabeth asked.

"I'm sure of it," Isabella said. "This must happen all the time. People get off the ship to sightsee and then miss the boat when it leaves. Denise and

Winston will probably show up any minute. They knew where we would be anchored tonight."

"You'd think they would have somehow gotten a message to us about what time to expect them."

"You know Winston," Isabella said. "He's not the most commonsensical person in the whole world. And when Denise is with him, she's just as bad. It might not occur to either one of them to call the ship and let us know."

Isabella was making sense, and Elizabeth felt some of her generalized misery over the state of everybody's affairs begin to ease up a little. "What about Leonardo?" she asked in small voice. What could Isabella possibly say about that situation to make it seem less heartbreaking?

"Noah's got himself a little competition. That's all." Isabella's light laughter actually forced Elizabeth's own lips into a smile.

"Don't worry about that," Isabella advised with a knowing wink. "Whether Noah and Alex realize it or not, this is the best thing that could happen to their relationship. It needed shaking up."

"Leonardo's breaking them up," Elizabeth protested. "Not shaking them up."

Isabella shrugged. "Everything will work out. You'll see."

"Not everything," Elizabeth said softly, turning away and looking out over the water. She squeezed her eyes shut to blink back the tears.

Then she wished she hadn't. Every time she closed her eyes, she saw Tom passionately kissing Nicole.

Once again the scene replayed itself in her mind. After arguing with Tom, Elizabeth had stepped out of the dining room to take a look around and get some air. Danny had had the same idea. So they'd both walked to the upper deck. And there were Tom and Nicole—locked in a passionate embrace.

Elizabeth had gasped, and Tom and Nicole had broken guiltily apart. In the horrible seconds that followed, Danny lunged for Tom, punching his best friend in the jaw.

Neither she nor Danny had spoken to Tom since.

"I know you're hurt," Isabella said softly. "But don't you think maybe you're blowing this out of proportion? You're really being hard on Tom. And so is Danny."

"I guess Danny and I think alike on this issue. Neither one of us likes lies. And we don't like liars, either," Elizabeth said shortly.

Isabella sighed. "Nobody likes liars. But you and Danny are both so . . . *rigid.*"

"If you caught Danny kissing somebody else, what would you do?" Elizabeth demanded.

"I would try to understand what had happened," Isabella said in a reasonable tone. "I know that people aren't perfect and sometimes they make mistakes and—"

"And you'd just smile sweetly and forgive him?"

"I'd try," Isabella said. "Because my relationship with Danny is important to me."

"Where is he, anyway?"

Isabella frowned. "Actually, I don't know. I haven't seen him since before dinner."

"Maybe he went over the side with Jessica," Elizabeth suggested morosely.

"Try to stay calm," Isabella said. "I'm sure Jessica's on the ship somewhere. She's probably skulking around trying to find her mystery man."

Jessica's mystery man was, indeed, extremely mysterious. In fact, Jessica was convinced he was her guardian angel. Over the past few weeks some tall, dark, broad-shouldered stranger had stepped in three times to save her life.

His latest act of heroism had been when Jessica fell overboard. He'd jumped in the water to save her, then disappeared as soon as he'd gotten her back on deck. Ever since, Jessica had been on a hunt for him, always positive that he was hiding around the next corner.

"I wish she would find him," Elizabeth muttered. "Or that he would find her. I'm tired of worrying about her and chasing her all over the place trying to keep her out of trouble."

"Then stop it," Isabella advised. "And try to enjoy yourself. Go to the dance on the Lido deck."

Elizabeth dropped her eyes. "I'm not really in the mood for a dance right now."

"The band is great. Listen."

The two girls leaned over the rail, letting the fresh ocean air cool their faces. Music from the ballroom on the Lido deck above them filtered down through the night. The DJ was playing a slow, romantic song that made Elizabeth's heart ache as she thought of Tom.

Resolutely she steeled herself against emotion. Tom was history. He'd made his choice when he put his arms around Nicole Riley. And now she had made hers.

"Elizabeth! I've been looking for you."

Elizabeth looked up as Todd Wilkins approached. There was a bittersweet smile on his handsome face. "Remember this tune?"

Elizabeth's mouth fell open in surprise. She did remember. "It's 'Old Times,'" she exclaimed. The romantic Johnny Buck ballad had been popular when she and Todd were in middle school together.

"As everyone knows, Elizabeth and I go back a long way," Todd explained to Isabella with a smile. "This was our song when we were in the second grade."

"No," Elizabeth corrected. "It was our song in the *sixth* grade. 'Pop Goes the Weasel' was our song in second grade. But please don't request it. I'm not up for a game of musical chairs."

Todd laughed and held out his hand to Elizabeth. "Then may I escort you to the Lido deck and have this dance?"

Elizabeth hesitated. "I really should find Jessica."

"Relax," Isabella instructed. "Jessica's probably at the dance herself, flirting outrageously with some gorgeous guy. I'm sure she's having a great time."

"Young lady, I know that American students tend to think that laws do not apply to them when they are on foreign soil. But I assure you, we take crime very seriously on this island."

The island's middle-aged police captain leaned back in his desk chair and folded his hands over his enormous stomach. An embossed nameplate on his desk identified him as Captain Jay.

He wore the same uniform the rest of the island policemen did—shorts with kneesocks and a military-style shirt.

The air in the little island jail building was hot and muggy. And the structure looked as if it hadn't been cleaned in months. Jessica wrinkled her nose in distaste when she noticed the dead bugs that had collected in the corners.

Over her head a low-hanging ceiling fan spun ineffectually in a desultory circle. The fan provided no air and was obviously placing a strain on the building's meager electrical reserves. Every other revolution of the blades produced a strange buzzing sound from the fan fixture, and every time the fan buzzed, the lights in the room dimmed.

The building consisted of a central lobby area

in which Captain Jay's desk was located. Just off the entrance was a hallway. On her way in, Jessica had caught a glimpse of the jail cells that lined the corridor.

"Yes, Ms. Wakefield," Captain Jay continued in his slightly threatening tone. "We take crime very seriously."

The two officers who had escorted Jessica from the cruise ship, unseen by her friends, stood on either side of Captain Jay's desk, staring at her with accusatory eyes.

Officer One stood with his hands behind his back. And Officer Two held a billy club. Every few moments he swung it upward with a practiced flourish and smacked it on the palm of his other hand. He looked like a man who was eager to do business.

"I told your men on the ship—you've made a mistake," Jessica said with a frown. "I haven't committed any crime."

Captain Jay lowered his head and looked at her over the rim of his glasses. Then he fumbled with some papers on his desk. After a pregnant pause, he picked up one page and scanned it as if refreshing himself with the contents. "Let us review the facts. According to Captain Avedon of the *Homecoming Queen*," he intoned, "a Mr. Jason Pierce and Ms. Nicole Riley are scheduled to be married onboard the *Homecoming Queen* tomorrow. You knew about this wedding?"

"Of course," Jessica agreed. "I'm invited to it. All my friends are."

Captain Jay gave her a long look and said nothing for a few moments. Then he consulted his papers again and cleared his throat. "Mr. Pierce has reported that a very valuable diamond ring was stolen from him. The ring had been given to a Mr. Danny Wyatt for safekeeping. He left it in his cabin when he disembarked from the ship to visit the island this afternoon. When he returned to the ship, the ring was gone." Captain Jay shook his head. "To steal a wedding ring is an awful crime."

"It's the worst thing I can think of," Jessica agreed. "But I didn't steal it."

The police captain picked up another piece of paper from his desk. "Do you know what this is?"

Jessica shook her head.

He handed it to her, and she scowled over the scrawled handwriting. There was a signature at the bottom, and the document was covered with stamps and embossed official seals.

"According to this statement, the ship's steward has no doubt that you're the thief."

Jessica shrugged. "He's wrong."

"Mr. Esteban has been employed on the *Homecoming Queen* for the past two years. He is a man of unimpeachable integrity."

Jessica looked closely at the page, trying to read the words written on it. "Well, he may be a man of unimpeachable integrity, but he's also a man of illegible penmanship." She giggled at her own joke and gave Captain Jay her sunniest smile. It was a smile that she knew from experience could melt the hardest male heart.

But Captain Jay's face remained implacable, and her laughter trailed off. Captain Jay exchanged a look with his henchmen, and Officer Two gave his billy club an even fancier twirl.

Captain Jay reached forward and plucked the paper from her fingers. "As outlined in this affidavit, Mr. Esteban swears that he saw you entering and leaving several cabins on the ship this afternoon. When he investigated further, it appeared to him that you had been rifling the drawers and examining the contents of other people's suitcases. Is this true?"

Jessica felt her face flushing. "Yes, but . . . you've got it all wrong."

"You admit that you were in several cabins?"

"Yes, but . . ."

"Do you admit also that you searched through the drawers and suitcases in those cabins?"

"Yes . . . but . . ."

"Ms. Wakefield. We are not stupid. It would be plain to the dullest observer that you are the culprit."

Jessica began to grow alarmed. Could they seriously believe she had stolen Jason's ring? It was ridiculous. It was absurd. But even she could tell the circumstantial evidence wasn't going to exonerate her.

She stood up and stamped her foot. "I swear, I *didn't* steal anything. I'm not a thief and I resent being treated like one. How dare you . . ."

She broke off as the two police officers lurched in her direction, ready to restrain her. But the police captain raised his hand, signaling them to stand back. "Sit down!" he thundered in a voice loud enough to shake the walls.

Jessica plopped back down in her seat, her heart hammering. Trying to remain calm, she breathed deeply.

She hadn't done anything wrong. She had nothing to fear. Jessica sat up, straightened her skirt, and lifted her chin. "I am not a thief," she repeated in a dignified tone.

The police captain raised a skeptical eyebrow. "Oh? Then what were you doing in those cabins?"

"I was looking for . . ."

"For?" he prompted.

She closed her mouth with a snap.

"Ms. Wakefield? What were you looking for?"

Jessica crossed her arms over her chest. "It's private."

"Ms. Wakefield. I must insist that you confide in me. You are accused of a very serious crime, and there seems to be a large body of damaging circumstantial evidence. If there is any mitigating circumstance of which I should be aware, now is the time to tell me."

Jessica glanced up at the depressing ceiling

fan. "I was looking for my guardian angel," she mumbled.

She lowered her gaze just in time to see Captain Jay roll his eyes.

"My guardian angel saved my life," she blurted. "I fell overboard and he pulled me out of the water. When I came to, I had a button in my hand. It was a button off a man's shirt. So I realized if I could find the shirt without the button, I could find the guy that belonged with the shirt. And that guy would be my guardian angel."

Captain Jay's stern face broke into a smile. "What a lovely story. It's like *Cinderella*," he said in a delighted tone of voice.

"That's right," Jessica agreed.

"Just like a fairy tale," he said, his eyes turning limpid.

"And so romantic," Policeman One said with a dreamy sigh.

"Very moving," Policeman Two agreed.

"That's right," Jessica said, relieved that her story had been so quickly understood and appreciated. "I was just looking for my Prince Charming."

"She was just looking for her Prince Charming," Captain Jay crooned.

Policeman Number One sighed again. "We should have known."

"Great. Then I guess we're all straightened out here. So unless you have any more questions, I'll be running along now and . . ."

15

Captain Jay's beatific smile immediately turned to a fierce glare. Policemen One and Two sprang forward and each took one of her arms.

"Hey!" Jessica protested as they pulled her to her feet.

"Now you listen to me," Captain Jay said, pointing his finger at her. "I've heard a lot of ridiculous excuses for thieving in my time, but that's the most absurd one I've heard this week." He leaned forward. "We've had our eye on you ever since you got to the Caribbean," he said ominously. "We had a report about a blonde pick-pocket on St. Lucia."

"You mean C. J. Kravitz from Yonkers? That was a mistake," she cried. "A misunderstanding. I thought he was my angel, and I grabbed him and . . ."

"Lock her up," Captain Jay ordered.

The two policemen began guiding Jessica around the corner and down the dusty stucco hallway. "But you can't lock me up. Listen to me! You've got the wrong person."

"We'll talk again when you're ready to tell us where the ring is," she heard Captain Jay say from the lobby area.

"But my boat leaves in an hour," she shouted as the policemen marched her briskly toward a cell.

"Tell it to your lawyer," Captain Jay replied.

"What lawyer?"

"We called the lawyer from the U.S. consulate before we went to the ship to get you," Policeman One replied. "We left a message for him to come here."

"You left a message? You didn't talk to him directly? Why not? Where is he? Try him again right now."

"No use. They think he went night fishing."

"When will he be back?"

Policeman One shrugged, opened a jail cell, and ushered her in. Jessica looked in horror at the bleak little cement block. "You're not really going to leave me in here, are you?"

She whirled around just in time to see the door to the cell swing shut.

Chapter Two

Todd's arms tightened around Elizabeth's waist, and she laid her cheek against his shoulder. It was just like old times, she reflected. It was just like high school, when she and Todd had been the perfect couple.

The dance on the Lido deck was crowded, and everywhere she looked she saw attractive, happy couples. Girls in gauzy evening dresses wore their hair up, and exotic blooms of every color were tucked inventively into French twists.

Most of the guys wore navy blazers and ties. But quite a few had brought white jackets and ties. The atmosphere was old-fashioned and romantic and . . . Elizabeth felt hot tears collecting in her eyes again.

She had thought it was like old times, but it wasn't. Not really. In high school, her heart had been light and she'd had no doubts at all that she was in love with Todd. Now she had all kinds of feelings that she didn't understand.

Todd's arms around her felt comforting. But she had no sense of delicious anticipation. Even so, she couldn't imagine wanting Tom's arms around her again. Not after the way he had treated her.

She was too angry and too hurt.

She caught sight of Tom across the crowd. Nicole stood at his elbow, holding a drink and talking rapidly and with great animation. Across the room Jason stood with a couple of his groomsmen, laughing loudly.

Nicole put her hand on Tom's arm, and he bent his dark, handsome head to better catch her words.

Elizabeth couldn't help groaning.

"Elizabeth?" Todd asked. "Is something wrong?"

"No," she answered in a muffled voice, pressing her face into his shoulder. "Everything's just fine." She swallowed the lump that was rising in her throat.

Tom plastered a smile on his face and made a good pretense of listening to Nicole. But the truth was, not one word was sinking in. He was really watching Elizabeth and Todd.

They were dancing close. And Elizabeth had just pressed her face against Todd's shoulder.

Waves of regret washed up and down Tom's body. The feeling was so intense it made the bottoms of his feet ache. How could he have done something so incredibly dumb and stupid? How could he have done so *many* dumb and stupid things—starting with the sleeping arrangements he had made for this trip?

Elizabeth had asked him to pick up the cruise tickets before the group left. When Tom had arrived at the travel agency, the travel agent said that all the roommate instructions Elizabeth had given her had gotten lost in the computer.

Tom had offered to reconstruct the information, and while he'd been figuring out who would probably want to room with whom, he'd let wishful thinking take the place of common sense. Somehow, he'd convinced himself that Elizabeth would probably want the two of them to share a cabin. So without even asking her, he had put them both in the same cabin.

As it turned out, that wasn't what she had in mind at all. She loved him, she had told him. But she wasn't ready to sleep with him. Her coolness had frustrated him—and damaged his male ego. Everything had gone downhill from there.

It was like the plot of some old movie. Nicole chattered on as he stared at her with unseeing eyes and an empty smile. In his mind, he reviewed the sequence of events as if he were a film critic.

Plot point one: Danny Wyatt announces over

breakfast that his best friend from high school, Jason Pierce, is getting married over spring break. The wedding is taking place on a six-day, seven-night Caribbean college cruise on a luxury ship called the Homecoming Queen. *Jason asks Danny to be his best man, but Danny can't afford to go.*

Plot point two: Elizabeth, heiress to the William White fortune, donates all the money to charity but keeps just enough to treat herself and all her friends to the best spring break ever—six days and seven nights in the Caribbean on the Homecoming Queen.

Tom took another bite of cookie. He noted that if he were sitting in a movie theater watching this story unfold on a screen two stories high, it would be right around here that he'd start to see the handwriting on the wall.

Plot point three: Onboard our hero, Tom, is stunned to realize that Jason Pierce's fiancée is Nicole Riley—a girl he dated in high school. He's even more surprised to discover that some of the old chemistry between them has lingered on.

It all seemed pretty formulaic when he stopped to think about it. Tom had been feeling ignored because Elizabeth seemed more interested in hanging out with Jessica than she was in spending any romantic time with him.

Nicole was feeling ignored because the minute Jason had reconnected with Danny, he'd seemed more interested in joking around with his

21

friends than he was in sharing quality time with his fiancée.

When Tom considered where both he and Nicole had been coming from, their kiss seemed totally predictable. Of course, Tom had regretted that kiss the moment his lips met Nicole's. But before he had a chance to pull away from her, Danny and Elizabeth had walked out on deck.

Tom rubbed his sore jaw, remembering Danny's punch. Elizabeth hadn't hit him. But he wished she had. It would have been far less painful than her cold and unforgiving silence.

So far, neither Danny nor Elizabeth had said a word to Jason about what they had seen. Elizabeth, Tom felt sure, would say nothing. She wouldn't think it was her place to get between Jason and Nicole.

But Danny?

Danny was taking a Twentieth-Century Ethics seminar, and he was developing a compulsion for truth telling that bordered on a mania. Would he tell Jason what he had seen?

Tom reached for another cookie and noticed Nicole's fingers fluttering nervously around her hair. The suspense was killing her and Tom both.

The lemon cookie tasted like dust in his mouth. The longer Tom stood staring at Elizabeth and Todd, the more twisted his insides became.

Tom had never liked Todd, even though Todd's quick thinking had saved Tom, Elizabeth, and their whole group of friends from a murder attempt by psychopath William White. Tom didn't trust him. Todd hadn't handled his status as freshman basketball star very well. He'd done a stint of heavy drinking, and he'd even gotten kicked off the basketball team because of a recruiting scandal.

All things considered, Tom thought Todd a very unsavory character. Exactly the kind of unsavory character that Elizabeth now thought Tom to be.

Tom regretted a lot of things in his life. But more than anything else, he regretted hurting Elizabeth. As tears welled up in his eyes, Tom watched Todd place his arm possessively around Elizabeth's smooth shoulders.

Lila Fowler put her brush down on the dresser and stared at herself in the mirror. Her face was pale, but her silver slip dress made her large blue eyes looked almost violet. Her dark hair hung around her shoulders in glamorous waves.

She turned and opened the closet door, gazing at her reflection in the full-length mirror. Her figure was perfect and her dress looked sensational. *She* looked sensational.

Lila closed her eyes and listened to the faint sound of the music on the Lido deck. She could picture herself dancing on the deck in Bruce's arms.

Immediately she opened her eyes and closed the closet door, despising herself for being so vain and childish. How could she stand there admiring her own reflection and thinking about Bruce when her husband, Tisiano, had been dead for only a few months?

When her brother-in-law, Leonardo, had arrived on the first night of the cruise and discovered that she was consoling herself with Bruce Patman, he had been extremely angry and upset.

Didn't Lila see how improper that was? he'd demanded. He insisted that it was too soon, much too soon, for her to even be *thinking* about love again. Not only did it dishonor the memory of Tisiano, but it was unwise for her to rush into a new relationship in such an emotionally fragile state. He'd maintained that grief and loneliness were clouding her ability to make mature and rational decisions.

Leonardo's attitude had been high-handed and even a little dictatorial, but he was so genuinely concerned about Lila's welfare, and so solicitous of her, that it had been impossible to take offense. And though Lila had never met her husband's brother, Tisiano had spoken of him so often that Lila felt as if she'd known him forever.

For Tisiano's sake Lila had forced herself to listen to Leonardo and to face the unpalatable truth: he was right. Pain and loss had clouded her judgment. How else could she explain the deep passion she felt for Bruce Patman—a guy she had known all her life but had disdained for most of it?

Until they had been stranded together in the mountains after a plane crash, Lila Fowler had never considered dating Bruce Patman. She'd thought he was rude, conceited, and inferior.

But somehow, on the top of a mountain with the specter of death looming over both of them, they had reached out to each other and tapped into deep and secret feelings that neither had suspected were there.

Or had they?

Had Lila mistaken her feelings? Did she love Bruce, or was the love she *thought* she felt for Bruce only a desperate attempt to embrace life in the shadow of death?

Leonardo had told her that she must mourn respectfully for "a decent interval." Then her heart would know for certain what her feelings were.

Suddenly the melody of "Old Times" brought back a flood of happier memories, and some of her sadness began to dissipate. Her feelings for Bruce might be jumbled and confused and all wrong, but he was still an old face from her past—and she was on a boat surrounded by old friends. The relationship she shared with several people on the boat was safe and comforting. She and Jessica had been best friends since they were children.

There was no reason not to go to the dance and enjoy the night and the music and the chance to wear a beautiful dress. Surely Leonardo didn't expect her to sit in her cabin alone until the cruise was over. He would want her to have *some* fun.

And she had told Bruce that they had to take a break. He would respect her feelings and not try to dance with her or hold her in his arms.

Lila felt a rush of anticipation. Her feet were moving quickly toward the door, and she was practically dancing as she grabbed her scarf from the bed.

She would find Jessica, and maybe Winston would have found his way back. And if Elizabeth wasn't busy dancing cheek to cheek with Tom or Todd or whomever she was with these days, they could all hang out together. It would be just like old times.

Gin-Yung Suh watched Todd and Elizabeth and felt something wet trickle down her cheek. Was the ceiling leaking?

She looked up, but nothing seemed to be dripping from above.

Could that mean that she, Gin-Yung Suh, sportswriter and self-proclaimed stoic, was really crying? Over Todd Wilkins?

Crying was something she did when the Yankees lost the World Series. Or an NFL strike canceled a Super Bowl. Or when a game went into overtime, and she knew that the terrific column she was going write about it would go unprinted and unread because by the time the game was over, her deadline would have been long gone.

Those were the sort of things that Gin-Yung cried about.

But crying over a guy? Never!

Before she could stop herself, her hand reflexively flew to her face and wiped her eyes.

She had thought that she and Todd had something special going. He'd certainly acted like it. Then Elizabeth Wakefield had broken up with Tom Watts, and she'd gone straight to Todd for consolation.

Gin-Yung had never seen a man do a one-hundred-and-eighty-degree turn so fast. He'd switched his allegiance from one girl to the other in the twinkling of Elizabeth Wakefield's eye. Gin-Yung was still having a hard time believing Todd was capable of doing such a crummy thing. He'd seemed like such a nice guy.

Maybe that's why it had happened. Maybe Todd was too nice a guy not to respond to the emotional needs of an old girlfriend in distress.

Gin-Yung felt a stab of anger at Elizabeth. She'd crooked her little finger and Todd had come running. He couldn't help himself, and Elizabeth had known it.

Gin-Yung watched them dance a little closer and bit her lower lip, scrutinizing Elizabeth. Romance was a game just like any other. One of the hallmarks of a good player was an ability to learn from the strengths of the other team.

As Gin-Yung watched through puffy eyes, Todd's hand stroked Elizabeth's bare back. Her tall, willowy shape looked like a model's in her black sequin halter dress. And her high heels made her long legs look even longer.

Gin-Yung dropped her gaze to her toes. She'd worn the same shoes for virtually every occasion—casual or dress—since she was in the fourth grade. Penny loafers. It had never occurred to her that she even needed another pair of shoes.

For that matter, she wore pretty much the same *clothes* for every occasion. Khaki pants, a white cotton shirt, and a comfortable blue blazer. For formal occasions she wore her khaki skirt instead of pants.

No wonder Elizabeth Wakefield had the advantage. Gin-Yung was going to need different gear if she was going to compete in this league.

She looked at her watch. She Sells, one of the ship's fanciest shops, stayed open until midnight. Gin-Yung had her dad's credit card. He'd said she should use it for emergencies. Wouldn't this count as an emergency?

In a sudden fit of self-consciousness, she put her punch glass down on a table and began backing out of the ballroom. This was an emergency, all right. A matter of life and death. She had to get out of here before she died of embarrassment.

28

Sheesh! she muttered to herself as she beat a hasty retreat. *How come nobody tells you these things?*

She had all kinds of friends. How come none of them had ever clued her in on this stuff? Maybe it was because most of her friends were guys. What did they know about clothes?

Once out of the ballroom, Gin-Yung hurried down the deck past the outdoor Café de Paris, where couples sat at romantic tables. Flickering votive candles lit their faces from below and the moon highlighted their hair. Stars twinkled in the black sky, and the ship's wake glowed white on the water's surface.

She saw several familiar faces at the café—couples who had slipped away from the dance for some private conversation. Alexandra Rollins, one of Todd's friends, and her new boyfriend, Leonardo, looked very cozy at their corner table.

Gin-Yung and Todd had spent several hours sitting at one of those tables. They'd talked mostly about sports, a subject on which both considered themselves authorities.

Gin-Yung felt another round of tears forming and fiercely choked them back. She doubled her speed as she headed for the stairwell that led to the shopping deck. The sooner she launched Operation Makeover, the better. "Omoomph!" she grunted in surprise as she collided with someone in the shadows.

"Sorry," the voice said quickly.

She peered through the dark to see whom she'd run into. "Noah! What are you doing here?"

He smiled tightly. "Just getting a breath of fresh air. Where are you going in such a hurry?" he inquired politely.

"To change my uniform," she answered, grabbing the rail, spinning around, and taking the stairs two at a time. "Don't go away! I'll be right back."

Yesterday she and Noah had done a little flirting. It wasn't anything serious. She knew that Noah was in love with Alex. And he knew that she had a major crush on Todd. But it wouldn't be a bad idea to do a little test marketing of the new Gin-Yung on someone besides Todd. Noah would make a perfect guinea pig.

Chapter
Three

Todd's hand moved again over Elizabeth's bare back. Her skin felt as soft and silky as it always had. But he was patting her back now more for comfort than anything else. She was crying. He could tell by the almost imperceptible tremble of her shoulders.

He felt like crying too. He'd felt miserable as he watched Gin-Yung leave the ballroom. Maybe someday, if he ever got his life straightened out, there was some chance he could put things back together with her.

But he could hardly drop Elizabeth when she was so upset and go running back to Gin-Yung. He'd already dropped Gin-Yung to go running back to Elizabeth.

He felt like kicking himself for handling things the way he had. He and Gin-Yung had started something meaningful. But when Elizabeth had dumped Tom Watts and turned to Todd, he had jumped at the chance to get back together with her. If only he'd thought through his emotions.

What would Gin-Yung think of him if he pulled the same stunt twice? She'd figure he was the most fickle guy in the whole world and that he wasn't capable of caring about *anybody's* feelings.

And no matter what he felt for Gin-Yung, he did still care about Elizabeth. So he was trying to do the decent thing and be here for her now.

She needed him. So he was smiling and dancing and flirting and trying to pretend that everything was the way it had been at the beginning of the school year, when they'd been madly in love with each other.

She was smiling and dancing and flirting back.

Maybe she was fooling herself, but Todd wasn't fooled at all. Elizabeth might not be ready to admit it, but the spark between them was gone. He didn't know why and he didn't know when, but somewhere along the line the physical attraction had disappeared. And they didn't seem to be able to get it back.

Maybe there had just been too much water under the bridge. Too much conflict between them. Maybe they had both arrived at college with completely unrealistic expectations and not nearly enough maturity.

Their freshman year had started out with so much hope and so much promise. They'd always been considered the perfect couple, and both had assumed that their love would last forever. Everything had always come so easily for both of them. Grades. Popularity. Extracurricular activities.

But all their perfection and hope had turned to vapor in a matter of weeks. Most of it had been his fault. Actually, *all* of it had been his fault.

He'd let his star status on the basketball team turn him into an egomaniac. He'd decided that if Elizabeth wasn't willing to sleep with him, he wasn't willing to wait.

So he'd broken up with her and started dating somebody else, while Elizabeth floundered around trying to figure out where she fit in the college scene.

But then their fortunes had reversed. He'd gotten thrown off the basketball team, and he'd turned to drinking and stopped going to classes.

And he'd watched Elizabeth fall deeply and passionately in love with Tom Watts, while Todd spiraled further and further downward. The only thing that had restored his self-esteem and gotten him started back on the right track was saving Elizabeth and all her friends from William White's insane, but extremely well-plotted murder attempt.

He looked down at the sexy glitter of sequins that lined the bodice of Elizabeth's dress. Her shoulders shook slightly again.

Todd pulled her closer, wishing he had some

words that would make her feel better. But he didn't. Whether she admitted it or not, he knew she was still grieving over the demise of her relationship with Tom.

Elizabeth Wakefield was beautiful, elegant, and sexy. On top of that, she was incredibly intelligent. But apparently she wasn't intelligent enough to realize that Tom Watts wasn't nearly good enough for her. And neither was Todd.

Isabella leaned against the rail with her arms crossed over her chest, watching the couples dance in the outside pavilion of the ballroom. Todd and Elizabeth swayed gracefully to the romantic music.

And on the other side of the ballroom Tom, Nicole, and Danny's best friend, Jason, stood around the punch bowl. Nicole's face wore a red flush and Tom was staring at his feet. But Jason didn't seem to notice that Tom and Nicole looked uncomfortable. He laughed and slapped Tom on the arm.

Jason was a real guy's guy, Isabella reflected. He loved hanging out with Danny and joking around with his buddies. In fact, she couldn't figure out why he wanted to get married. He didn't seem to be ready. And apparently Nicole wasn't ready either. If she were, she wouldn't have been kissing Tom.

Still, it was none of Isabella's business. And none of Danny's, either.

Isabella felt a faint flicker of worry. Had she remembered to lock her cabin door? After Danny had told her and Jason that the ring Jason had given him for safekeeping had been stolen, she had vowed to be extra cautious.

The captain had asked them to say nothing of the theft until he and the island authorities had had time to investigate, but Isabella made a mental note to warn her friends that they would be wise to lock up their valuables from now on.

Isabella tapped her foot impatiently. Where was Danny, anyway? She'd been looking forward to tonight's dance ever since she'd read about the cruise. She was wearing a long black dress with a fluted skirt that she had bought especially for the cruise. The graceful hem swirled romantically around her ankles—but her outfit was going to go to waste if Danny didn't show up for the dance.

The band struck up one of Isabella's favorite songs, "Dancing with You," and she was still without a dancing partner. "All right, Mr. Wyatt," she muttered, hurrying past the Café de Paris. "Wherever you are, and whatever you're doing, it's not as important as dancing with me."

Isabella tilted her head back to admire the spectacular moon. She closed her eyes, wishing that Danny were standing beside her, holding her in his arms and bending his head over hers in a romantic kiss. That's what she had envisioned when they found out they were going on a cruise. But they hadn't exchanged as much as one romantic kiss in the moonlight yet.

They had hardly had two minutes alone since they got on the ship. And when they did have two minutes, they argued.

Ever since that fateful second night when Danny had seen Tom kissing Jason's fiancée, he'd been impossible. He was surly, grumpy, and judgmental.

She opened her eyes and took a last longing look at the glowing moon. She was going to search the entire *Homecoming Queen* for Danny.

Isabella descended the stairs to check the shopping area on the second level. Most of the shops were closed, but a few remained open, and Isabella quickly circled the ship's mall.

Clearly Danny wasn't shopping. And he wasn't at the newsstand either.

Hmmm, she thought. *If I were Danny and I was in a bad mood, where would I be?*

Bowling, maybe?

On the third deck she poked her head into the bowling alley.

It was empty.

She hurried down to the other end of the corridor and looked through the window of the lounge. Two guys sat playing cards and eating a pizza. But neither one of them was Danny.

As a last resort she went down to the bottom level. Maybe he had gone back to his cabin to sulk.

But when she knocked on his door, there was no answer.

Isabella sighed heavily. Obviously Danny didn't want to be found. So she might as well return to the ballroom and stand there like a wallflower while everybody else had a wonderful time.

On her way up the stairs she heard a cough from the other side of a supply closet door. She paused, unsure of what to do. The cleaning crews were all finished by this time of night. Who could be in the supply closet?

She jerked open the door. "Danny!"

He was sitting on a box of equipment, with his chin resting in his hand.

"What are you doing in here?" she demanded. "I've been looking all over for you. The dance started ages ago."

"I know," Danny said glumly. "I'm hiding."

"From who?"

"From Jason. I'm too ashamed to face him." Danny shot her a sheepish look. "I lied to him."

Isabella took a deep breath, determined not to spoil the evening completely by losing her temper. She wiped some dust from the box on which he sat and perched beside him. "Danny," she said softly. "We've been over this and over this. You saw Tom Watts and Nicole Riley kissing. But there's no law that says you have to tell everything you know. I wouldn't call not telling Jason that you saw Tom and Nicole kissing *lying*. I'd call it minding your own business. If you stay out of it, things might work out all right. If you go sticking your nose in where it doesn't belong, you'll just cause more trouble."

"That's not the lie I'm talking about. I told him *another* lie. A *real* lie."

"What are you talking about?"

Shamefaced, Danny reached into the pocket of his jacket and removed something. "Here," he said, putting it into Isabella's hand. "This is what I'm talking about."

Isabella's other hand flew to her mouth and she gasped. A beautiful ring sparkled in her palm, reflecting the dim light from the corridor. "Danny! Is this Jason's ring?"

Danny nodded. "Yep! That's the famous Pierce family ring. The one that's been handed down through four generations of Pierce women."

"Oh, thank goodness. You found it? That's great. Why haven't you told him? Where did you find it? Whoever stole it must have—"

"Nobody stole it," Danny said curtly, cutting her off. "I've had it all the time. But when Jason walked into my cabin and said he wanted to marry Nicole right then and there, I knew I had to stop him. So I told him the ring had been stolen from my cabin. You know how sentimental he is about the ring. I was hoping he wouldn't want to get married without it. I thought it would buy a little time. And maybe if they have a little more

38

time, they'll realize they can't get married."

"Why can't they get married?" Isabella asked.

"Jason's too young," Danny said gravely.

"That's Jason's business. If he thinks he's old enough to get married, then it's not up to you to tell him that he isn't."

"But Jason can't marry Nicole. Not if she's in love with Tom."

"But you don't know she's in love with Tom," Isabella argued in a voice of mounting frustration. "You saw them kissing. That's all. Just because they were kissing doesn't mean they're in love. You're totally overreacting."

"And I think you're totally underreacting," Danny insisted. "She was sure kissing him like she was in love with him. And he was kissing her back the same way."

"It's still none of your business," Isabella insisted. "And believe me, if you tell Jason, he won't thank you. Ten to one he'll be mad at you for telling him something he doesn't want to know. It's the old shoot-the-messenger syndrome."

"I can't believe it. I just can't believe my best friend, Tom Watts, could turn out to be such a rotten cheating jerk."

"Well, I'll bet he'd be surprised to know you lied to Jason about this ring," Isabella retorted.

"Hey! *I* lied for a good reason."

"Oh! So now it's okay to lie for a good reason," she challenged, her patience beginning to wear thin. "What happened to the famous Wyatt sense of ethics, where right is right and wrong is wrong and there's nothing in the middle?"

Danny clutched his head with his hands. "Stop trying to confuse me. I'm trying to do the right thing—but I can't figure out what it is."

"Why don't you think it over while we dance in the moonlight?" she suggested, changing tactics by switching her tone from accusatory to seductive. If he couldn't be guilt-tripped into dancing with her, maybe he could be coaxed.

Danny shook his head. "No. This messenger is staying right here until I've thought this thing through and come up with the ethical solution."

She jumped to her feet and stamped one foot on the floor. Her black dress shimmered around her as her body shook with indignation. "All right, then, Danny Wyatt," she shouted. "You just sit in the dark by yourself. But I'm telling you right here and now—I'm sick and tired of you obsessing over everybody else's love life when ours stinks!"

"Isabella!" Danny stared at her, his mouth gaping. Isabella knew he wasn't used to seeing her lose her temper. But it was time he understood that she hadn't come on this cruise to sit in a storage room while Danny pondered the finer points of contemporary ethics.

"Be a man, why don't you? Tell Jason the truth about the ring, and then clear out of his love life. *That's* obviously the ethical thing to do. And I didn't have to spend an hour sitting in a dirty supply closet to figure it out."

"Isabella! Wait!"

But Isabella didn't wait to hear what he had to say. She slammed the door shut behind her and marched down the hall toward her cabin. She was through being Miss Sunshine and trying to make light of all the difficulties. Elizabeth was right. This cruise was a total disaster. She'd been looking forward to six days and seven nights of romance with Danny.

But all he'd done since they got here was hang out with Jason, practically kill her with fear while he played hero going after a pickpocket, and sulk because he'd seen one of his best friends kissing the fiancée of his other best friend.

"I wish I'd just stuck to my original plan for spring break and gone home," she muttered, entering her cabin and turning on the light.

She sighed, staring at the empty bed that belonged to Denise Waters. Nothing on the bed or the dresser had been moved. Obviously Denise wasn't back.

Isabella walked out of the cabin again, not bothering to lock the door. The information desk on deck two was open twenty-four hours a day. Maybe a message was there from Denise.

Isabella took the stairs and made her way into the main lounge area. The dim lighting gave the deserted interior deck an eerie glow, and the potted palms looked as dispirited as Isabella felt.

A sleepy clerk sat behind the counter, reading a newspaper.

"Excuse me," Isabella began.

He immediately lowered the newspaper and jumped to his feet. "Yes, miss. May I help you?"

"Is there any message for Isabella Ricci or for anybody from either Denise Waters or Winston Egbert?"

The clerk frowned, then snapped his fingers. "The couple that were left behind on St. Lucia. No, I'm sorry. There aren't any messages from them."

"But I talked to Captain Avedon earlier," she said. "He told me it would be very simple for them to catch a boat to this island and catch up with the ship."

The clerk consulted his watch. "Well, they don't have much time. We'll be sailing soon."

"If they miss this connection, what will they do?" Isabella asked, her voice catching.

The clerk brightened. "There's Captain Avedon. Why don't you ask him?"

Isabella turned and saw the captain walking briskly through the lobby with two of his staff behind him. "Captain Avedon!" she cried.

His face was stern and he seemed extremely preoccupied, but he paused and listened while she explained that there was still no sign of Denise and Winston. "What do we do now?" she asked in a worried tone.

Captain Avedon gave her a tight-lipped smile.

"Believe me, every island is equipped to deal with exactly this type of difficulty. If your friends *wanted* to catch up with the boat, they would have."

"Then where are they?"

"I have no idea," Captain Avedon said dryly. "But your group doesn't seem to be having a very good time together. Perhaps they decided they would have more fun on their own. Now if you'll excuse me, I have some pressing business."

Isabella watched him walk away, torn between anger and tears. Captain Avedon had clearly had enough of the SVU group's antics. And while his response had been rude, it was heartbreakingly on target. Still, she couldn't believe that Winston and Denise had simply opted to go off somewhere on their own. They would have called or sent a wire or something.

Isabella trudged back to her cabin and flopped down on the bed. It was lonely without Denise.

It was lonely without Danny.

It was lonely, period.

She rolled over on her back and groaned. "Why didn't I go home with a stack of good books?"

"Keep bailing!" Winston urged. "Keep bailing."

"I'm bailing. I'm bailing," Denise panted.

"I can't believe this," Winston exclaimed. "Like we don't have enough problems already. Our motor's kaput. We don't have food or water.

We're lost. We've got no paddle. And now our boat is leaking."

"We'll be okay," Denise assured him, sloshing water out of the bottom of the tiny boat with two hands. They had rented it on St. Lucia when they had missed the ship, planning to motor to the *Homecoming Queen*'s next port of call. But somewhere in the vast ocean they had taken a wrong turn, spent an unforgettably horrible night on some tiny island with no phone service, and then set out again this morning, hoping to catch up with their friends.

But so far they hadn't caught even a glimpse of the boat. And Murphy's law seemed to be plotting their course. Everything that could go wrong was going wrong.

"But how long can we keep this up?" Winston asked through cracked lips. He scooped some water out of the bottom of the boat and felt his arm muscles beginning to shake with the effort. Every movement of his arm caused his sunburned shoulders to ache.

Thank goodness, it was finally night. The afternoon sun had scorched his pale skin to a crisp. Denise was more olive skinned, but even her brown cheeks and nose had looked bright red by the time the sun went down.

"We'll keep it up until we spot help or help spots us," Denise said grimly.

Chapter Four

"Good catch today," Jean Martin said happily to Bryan Nelson. The huge pile of freshly caught fish glittered like silver in the moonlight. The surface of the water made a gentle smacking sound against the side of the boat as Jean brought it closer to the dock nearest the fish market. "Best catch in a long time." He smiled at Bryan. "I think maybe you are bringing me good luck."

Bryan smiled and lifted his shoulder, wiping the sweat from his brow with the sleeve of his SVU T-shirt. "I'm glad I can make somebody happy," he replied ruefully.

Jean leaned over and slapped him on the shoulder. "Come on, Bryan. This is the Caribbean. Don't worry. Be happy."

"How can I be happy when the woman I love is living it up without me? Nina's probably dancing in the arms of Dr. Daniels right now." He shook his head. "I never should have left the ship."

When Bryan had stalked angrily off the *Homecoming Queen,* he'd planned to catch a plane back to California and go straight back to the SVU campus. There was only one problem.

There was no airstrip.

There was no boat off the island, either—at least, not one that Bryan would get in. Denise and Winston had gotten left behind accidentally. They had rented a small boat, intending to catch up with the ship at the next island. That island had an airstrip, they assured him. He could catch a plane back to California.

But at the last minute Bryan's water phobia had kicked in and he hadn't been able to force himself into the little boat. So Denise and Winston had left without him, promising to send a helicopter back for him.

As soon as they were gone, Bryan discovered that he had been pickpocketed. Which meant he was marooned in a strange place with not one penny in his pocket. Luckily Bryan had run into Jean Martin, a young fisherman.

Jean had offered him food and a place to stay in exchange for work. The boys had gotten off to a bad start when Bryan had revealed that he was afraid of the water. Jean had insisted that he didn't have enough money to feed and house someone who was afraid to get in the ocean. And he had employed some pretty rough techniques to teach Bryan to swim.

He'd simply thrown him into the water.

Once Bryan had gotten over his fear of the water and learned to swim, he discovered that he enjoyed the island life—even the fishing and the water.

It sure beat his grueling academic schedule and the huge responsibility of heading up one of the biggest Black Student Unions in the state.

But he was beginning to appreciate the difficulties of Jean's life. Hours and hours of hard, backbreaking work would sometimes produce a small catch and an even smaller price.

The island offered few other employment opportunities. So Jean was hoping to leave the island next fall and attend college.

Jean's girlfriend was already in school. She wrote to Jean regularly, encouraging him to try to get some kind of scholarship. The more education he had, she had told him, the better his chances of success.

At first Jean had resisted. He was a fisherman. His father had been a fisherman. His grandfather had been a fisherman. If he got an education, would he be turning his back on an important tradition?

But then he'd realized that if he wanted a future with his girlfriend, he was going to have to at least try to do things differently. To learn something new. And he had been working hard on an essay that he hoped would help him win a scholarship to college.

The small generator that ran the pump on Jean's boat began to smoke and sputter.

"See if you can fix that, will you?" Jean asked as he lifted a huge net and folded it neatly on the side of the deck.

"Sure thing," Bryan answered with a grin. He reached for Jean's toolbox, located the appropriate-size screwdriver, and began tinkering with the old generator the way Jean Martin had taught him. In a matter of moments he had the problem under control.

Motors were pretty interesting things, Bryan had decided. In fact, motors were a lot like people. Once you figured out what made them tick, it was a lot easier to live with them.

Bryan's short time with Jean had taught Bryan a thing or two about motors—and life. He'd learned to be grateful for the things he had always taken for granted—his education and the job opportunities that were ahead of him.

He'd taken Nina Harper for granted, too. And that had been a big mistake. For some reason, he'd felt as if it was okay to insist that she do everything his way. He'd felt as if his masculine dignity would be compromised by doing things *her* way.

So he'd gotten her involved with meetings,

rallies, and envelope-stuffing parties. And he had refused to go jogging or dancing or in-line skating with her—even though those things were as important to her as the BSU was to him.

Bryan closed his eyes and tried to ignore the aching sensation around his heart and the lump that was rising in his throat. Why had he acted like such an idiot?

"Come on, Bryan," Jean urged in his gentle Caribbean accent. "The sooner we get finished here, the sooner we can get cleaned up and get something to eat."

Bryan hurried to help Jean transfer the fish to large crates and ice it down so that it would stay fresh until it got to the market.

"So," Jean Martin said, packing down the shaved ice with a pair of heavy work gloves. "It's nice to finish with a big success. Right?"

"Finish? What do you mean?"

Jean smiled. "I looked at your brochure. Tonight the *Homecoming Queen* leaves the island of Juma. That means tomorrow, the ship won't be too far away. You can catch up and rejoin your friends."

Bryan frowned. Yesterday he'd felt confident and enthusiastic about himself. He'd even thought about trying to learn to water-ski and had fantasized about skiing up to the ship to impress Nina.

But now that he was facing the real possibility of seeing her again, he realized there was probably no reason to go back to the cruise. Even before he'd left, the handsome ship's doctor had done a pretty good job of sweeping Nina off her feet. By now, Bryan wouldn't have a chance. "I've been thinking about that," he said uneasily. "Maybe going back to the ship isn't such a great idea. I think I'd rather stay here till the end of spring break. You can use another pair of hands on the boat. And I'm having fun here."

Jean smiled but said nothing.

Another boat pulled up next to Jean and the two old fishermen in it gave the boys a hearty greeting. "Good fishing?" one of them asked.

Jean nodded and pointed toward the crates full of fish. "Best catch in weeks," he replied.

The old man in the next boat smiled. "Us too. The sea was generous today." Bryan watched the old man as he coiled the ropes of the boat. His fingers were gnarled and callused from hard work. But his hands were strong and confident.

Jean had that same kind of confidence, Bryan realized. Despite the harsh conditions of his life, his uncertain future, and the tremendous economic gulf that separated him from the privileged and the educated, he carried himself with a relaxed self-assurance. He was Bryan's age. But he had the dignity of a man.

Bryan sighed inwardly. He was always afraid of looking foolish. Of looking indecisive. Of looking unmanly.

He wanted to be like Jean. But if he went back and Nina wouldn't speak to him, he would look like a jerk. "Yeah, I think I'll stay here," Bryan said softly, knowing as he said it that he was taking the boy's way out.

"Thank you, Rich." Nina gave the doctor her brightest smile as she took the glass of punch from him. He smiled back and Nina sighed. Dr. Richard Daniels looked as if he had just stepped off the set of *Internal Medicine,* her mother's favorite soap opera—not that her mother spent much time in front of the television set.

In fact, Nina wished her mother could be here to see her with this great guy. Nina's mother liked people who were "success oriented."

For that matter, so did Nina.

Not that Bryan wasn't successful. He was. But Bryan insisted on doing everything the hard way. He always had to prove himself by going against the grain.

Rich Daniels had graduated at the top of his class in medical school and then snagged this great job with the cruise line.

He worked hard, he told her. But he played hard too. Just like her.

"Drink up," Rich urged, tapping his feet to the music. "I love to dance, and this is one of my favorite songs."

Dr. Daniels was handsome, charming, brilliant,

51

and rich, a gentleman and a fabulous dancer. There was only one problem. . . .

"You know," he said, flashing her his melting smile as he twirled her out onto the floor, "you're one of the very few women I've had who can keep up with me. I studied with the best dancing teachers in the Northeast and I'm as good on the dance floor as I am in the water, or on the back of a horse, or behind the wheel of a fast European car." He laughed. "I don't think there are too many men who can say that. Do you?"

. . . He was a jerk.

Alex sat at a white wrought-iron table in the Café de Paris and sipped her espresso. Across from her Leonardo di Mondicci's dark face had a beautiful golden glow and an aristocratic quality. His finely chiseled lips and nose and tousled dark hair made him look as if he had just stepped off the ceiling of an Italian cathedral.

He was the most beautiful man she had ever met. And one of the most elegant. And the most passionate. And the richest.

Music floated toward them, and over their heads a full moon hung from the sky like an old-fashioned lamp, casting a romantic light over the entire outdoor café.

"Modeling is like acting, but five thousand times more exciting," he said in an eager voice. He leaned forward and took the lemon slice from the dish beneath Alex's mineral water and began to rub it against the rim of the cup. "Do this," he said in his gentle Italian accent. "So that you can taste the flavor of the lemon while you sip the water. That is how we do it in Italy."

She took a sip and wrinkled her nose. She preferred coffee or tea to the bitter mineral water Leonardo always ordered for her. But Leonardo told her that she should avoid coffee and tea because they would stain her teeth.

He caught the gesture and laughed. "You will get used to it," he assured her. "In Italy, all the models practically live on mineral water. Drink coffee only on the days you are modeling. Then you will want the strong coffee to wake you up and give you energy on the runway."

Alexandra shivered, and a trail of goose bumps raced up her spine. Leonardo seemed to be taking it for granted that she would be returning to Italy with him. "Do you really think I have a chance at modeling?" she asked.

Leonardo put his small coffee cup down with a loud rattle. He leaned forward and took her hand, holding it tightly in his. "Oh, yes. Say you will come to Italy with me. Say yes. If you will, I promise you will be a supermodel," he breathed. "I will make you one."

"Doesn't it take a lot of training and luck and . . ."

"Training? Yes. I will give you training. The

modeling agency I own has been in business for years. We have excellent teachers, excellent photographers, hairdressers, everything. Luck?" He grinned and pointed to his chest with his free hand. "You do not need luck as long as you have me. I will see to everything. The trips to Paris for the shows in the spring. The bookings in Milan. The swimsuit issue of *American Sports*."

Alex closed her eyes. She'd always dreamed about a fairy godmother who would appear and make all her wishes come true. But Leonardo was fifty times better. A handsome Italian who owned a modeling agency and was absolutely crazy about her.

He didn't seem to have any trouble calling her Alexandra either, she thought with a flicker of resentment. All through high school, Alex had been Enid Rollins. More accurately, *plain* Enid Rollins.

When she'd gotten to Sweet Valley University, she'd changed her name to Alexandra and tried to glamorize herself and her lifestyle. The results had been sort of disastrous. She'd done way too much heavy drinking and wound up alienating friends, losing boyfriends, and looking pretty stupid. Her life had fallen apart and shattered into a million pieces.

Then she'd met Noah, a quiet, sweet, and extremely understanding psychology major. He'd helped her put herself back together. But once Humpty-Dumpty had been reassembled, she looked a whole lot more like plain old Enid than Alexandra.

She *felt* a whole lot more like plain old Enid, too.

As much as she loved Noah, she resented him for making her feel that way. But she didn't know how to tell him that. Because the only way he could make her feel like a different woman was to be a different man. And the last thing she wanted was for him to be a different man.

Then Leonardo had come along. He clearly regarded Alex as the glamorous creature she had always wanted to be. Furthermore, he was standing by with his magic wand, waiting to make her a top model on the international fashion scene.

She could imagine herself at the clubs of Europe, having her picture taken with rock stars and movie people and lunching in trendy restaurants with people she had read about in magazines.

"Alessandra!" she heard Leonardo prompt. "Are you listening to what I'm telling you?"

Alex put down her coffee cup and smiled, tilting her head so that her curls swirled around her and caught the beams of moonlight. "I'm sorry. I think I was daydreaming."

"Dreams are good," he said approvingly. "You are a girl who should have very big dreams. Because I can make those dreams come true."

He lifted his hands and peered through them

as if they were a frame. "Yes," he whispered, almost to himself. "Yes. You have it. You definitely have it. I think for next fall we'll contact the younger designers. The avant-garde. You can carry it off and they always get a lot of press because they attract show-business types. You'll get a lot of publicity."

He leaned forward and his warm hand traveled up her arm, caressed her shoulder, and then stroked her cheek. His eyes were half shut and his hand began to move with a slow and sensual languor.

Alex's heart was thumping with excitement. There was nothing lazy or disinterested in the touch. Beneath his heavy-lidded eyes, there was something possessive and volcanic. Her breathing began to grow shallow and rapid.

Leonardo was offering all the things she had ever wanted—glamour, popularity, fame, and admiration. But more important, he was offering her passion.

As his fingers caressed the curly tendrils around her ear, she realized that it was passion she had been craving for so long.

But when she closed her eyes, Leonardo's sensuous movie star face disappeared and was replaced by Noah's all-American frank gaze, watching her from behind his long lashes.

There was warmth and admiration and yes, maybe even love from Noah, but no passion.

He didn't seem to be capable of it. Of course he cared about her. She knew that. But passion just didn't seem to be in Noah's emotional repertoire.

Her heart ached and felt as if it were going to break in two. On the one hand, she felt like Sleeping Beauty. Someone who had been asleep and awakened with a kiss.

On the other hand, she felt like a moron. Because even though she was being wooed by a prince named Leonardo, she couldn't stop thinking about a frog named Noah.

"Excuse me," she said, suddenly determined to find her frog and get a couple of things straight. Maybe she was wrong about him. Before she made any big decisions, she wanted to be very, very sure.

Noah leaned back farther into the shadows, burying his head in his hands. Hot tears rolled down his cheeks. He'd heard every word. And every word had pricked his heart like a lance.

He'd lost Alex. That was all there was to it. And he couldn't hide from it anymore. Leonardo had swept her off her feet.

How could Noah ever compete with a guy like that? A guy who was older, better looking, and richer. A guy who owned a modeling agency and was offering to make Alex an international superstar in the fashion world.

All Noah could give her was a shoulder to cry on and a sympathetic ear. He couldn't give her a career or money or trips to exotic places. He couldn't even give her advice—he didn't have his degree yet.

He'd been worried for a long time that he was too dull a guy for Alex and that he couldn't make her happy. She was exciting and spontaneous. She was a girl who would never feel happy if she felt trapped. So Noah had tried to give her lots of space and not come on too strong. But it hadn't worked. He'd given her all the breathing room he could, but the sparks still weren't flying. At least not in his direction. But she'd been drawn to Leonardo like a magnet. And why wouldn't she be? He was just as glamorous and exotic as she was.

"I've got to pull myself together," he muttered, turning away toward the rail and moving down the deck. He couldn't bear to watch them together any longer.

Halfway down the deck, he froze. She was walking toward him, and she looked like the glamorous model Leonardo wanted to make her. He'd never seen a woman look so beautiful. "Noah," she said softly. "I was hoping to find you."

He cleared his throat and took a step back so she wouldn't see that his eyes were red and swollen.

She stepped closer and he stepped back again.

58

On his best day, he couldn't compete with a guy like Leonardo. And he sure couldn't expect to keep Alex's respect if she saw him weeping like a child. "Having a nice time?" he managed to say, keeping the raspy note out of his voice.

"Yes. I just . . . I just thought we could talk. I wanted to, uh . . ."

You want to tell me it's over, but don't know how to do it, he finished for her mentally. Alex was a sweet girl, and she knew he cared about her. She'd have a hard time telling him to get lost.

Well, he didn't want to cause her any trouble. And he didn't want to stand in her way. The least he could do for the woman he loved was to make things as easy as possible for her.

"Look, Alex," he began. "I think we both know that we're not right for each other . . ."

. . . and I'm not the least bit in love with you, she finished for him. "I understand what you're trying to say," she managed to choke. "You don't have to add anything else."

"You deserve better than a mild-mannered psych major." When he gave her a faint smile, it was all Alex could do not to burst into tears. It especially hurt that he was literally *backing* away from her.

Alex didn't need Noah to go into gory detail about why he wasn't interested in having a passionate relationship with her. She already knew

59

that he was a serious guy who was serious about school and everything else. Noah was down to earth, and he was always in control. A less-than-perfect girl like Alex didn't fit into his lifestyle. When they went to his friends' parties together, she always stood out like a sore thumb. She embarrassed him. But he was just too nice to say it.

"And you deserve somebody who . . . who . . ." Alex forced herself to smile. "Someone who fits in with your life better than I do." She turned away before her lips began to tremble and walked quickly in the opposite direction. Her high heels made a clacking sound on the deck and her hair flew in the night air, almost blinding her.

Suddenly she stumbled forward. A pair of strong arms caught her.

"Alessandra!" she heard Leonardo exclaim in a deep voice. "I got worried and came to look for you." He pushed her hair away from her face. Immediately his own face clouded with concern. "Alessandra, darling, you are upset?"

She shook her head. "No," she said softly. "No. I . . ."

He smiled. "Of course you are upset. Why not? There is so much to take in at once. Your life is going to change so dramatically. You will be a star. But you will grow to like it. You will also grow to like me—I hope." He pulled her toward him and kissed her lips until her knees grew weak.

After several moments he released her and lifted

one eyebrow. "So? Is it yes? Or no? Will you come to Italy with me and become a supermodel? Or go back to Sweet Valley University and be a . . ." He trailed off and laughed. Because the end of the sentence was so obvious. If she went back to Sweet Valley University, she'd be nothing. Absolutely nothing. She'd be *plain old Enid Rollins*, the girl she was determined never to be again.

As soon as he got back to the far end of the deck, Noah blew his nose, dried his eyes, and stuffed his bandanna back into his pocket. There was a brisk wind coming off the sea, and the ocean spray stung his face.

"What are you still doing out here by yourself?"

Noah turned in surprise and saw Gin-Yung staring at him.

He shook his head, momentarily at a loss for words. "I'm just getting some air," he said in a hoarse tone.

"Bull," she said. "You're crying."

"I am not," Noah argued.

"Sure you are. Your eyes are red and—"

"It's the salt air," he said curtly.

She nodded. "Yeah, right. And it's got nothing whatsoever to do with the fact that Alex's spent most of the evening in the café holding hands with that Italian guy."

He turned and put one hand on his hip. "Are

61

you here to try to comfort me or pour salt in the wound?" he demanded.

She held up her hands in a gesture of surrender. "Sorry, tact was never my best sport. Believe it or not, I came over to try to make you feel better."

"I hate to burst your bubble, but it's not working."

"Too bad I'm a sportswriter and not a gossip columnist," she commented, leaning next to him. "This would be a great story. Just think of the headline: DEAD COUNT'S BROTHER DESTROYS FOWLER HEIRESS'S ROMANCE—AND AN INNOCENT PSYCH MAJOR SUFFERS IN THE PROCESS."

"Yeah, that guy seems to have a talent for killing romance—unless it's his own," Noah remarked mournfully.

"He's not the only one," Gin-Yung said sourly. "Whatever it was I had going with Todd went down the drain as soon as Elizabeth let him know she was available again."

"I don't think anybody's romance is still on track."

"Well, Jason and Nicole are still engaged," she pointed out. "And Danny and Isabella seem pretty solid. Other than that, though . . ." She shrugged and stared at her feet.

"Hey," Noah said, putting an arm around her shoulders. "Don't let me get you down. You're a beautiful girl and a great sportswriter."

Noah looked closely at Gin-Yung, noticing for the first time that she'd shed her khaki pants and button-down shirts in favor of a very feminine dress. Small and petite, she looked cute in the fancy pink dress. Noah couldn't help grinning to himself. Gin-Yung wasn't exactly the kind of girl he expected to see in that kind of getup.

"Excuse me for making a personal remark, but I like your . . ." He was momentarily stumped and gestured toward her dress. "Does this, uh, outfit have some kind of name?"

"It's a pouf dress," she said, tugging at the bodice and checking the skirt. "And if you laugh, I'll punch you."

"I wouldn't laugh." He smiled. "It's very becoming. And you're way too sweet a girl to laugh at."

Gin-Yung leaned against the rail and gave him a friendly pat on the shoulder. "You're a great guy," she said quietly. "You've only got one fault." She stared fixedly at the sleeve of his coat.

"What? Lint?"

She laughed. "No, silly. You're wearing your heart on your sleeve. My great-granddad always told me it was very foolish to wear your heart on your sleeve."

"What do you think your great-granddad would suggest?"

"I think he would suggest that we come up with a game plan to get what we want."

Noah nodded. "I'll be happy to help you with

your game plan. But I'm already out of the game."

"Hey! You're down, not out," she insisted. "So I think that you and I should go to the dance. We'll act like we're having a great time and we don't care what Todd or Alex is doing. And if we try hard enough, who knows, we might actually wind up having a good time." She tugged at the bodice of her dress again.

Noah took out his bandanna, wiped his eyes one more time, and then replaced it before offering Gin-Yung his arm. "Okay, Coach. We'll give it a try. Here's my sleeve," he said with a smile. "Guaranteed heart-free."

Chapter Five

Bruce Patman paced up and down the deck, feeling totally distraught. This was horrible. Unbelievably, excruciatingly horrible. It was as if Lila had just cut him completely out of her life. She wouldn't talk to him. She wouldn't take his phone calls. She refused to accept the flowers he sent to her cabin. And if she saw him approaching, she turned around and ran in the other direction.

And it was all because of Leonardo, the brother of Lila's late husband. On the second night of the cruise he had landed in a helicopter on the deck of the *Homecoming Queen,* stepped out into the moonlight, and practically given Lila a heart attack. *Tisiano,* she had screamed, thinking it was the apparition of an enraged and jealous dead husband. She'd fainted in Bruce's arms. Since then, his relationship with Lila had been reduced to nothing.

He thrust his hands down in his pockets, thinking hard. Maybe the thing to do was to act, not react. Maybe he should take the bull by the horns and aggressively try to work this thing out with Leonardo—man to man.

Yeah. That was exactly the right thing to do. Once Bruce explained things to Leonardo and told him that he and Lila had known each other since grammar school, maybe he'd ease up on the old-world brother-in-law-from-hell routine.

Bruce felt better already. He headed down the stairs to the Lido deck, where the Café de Paris was located. The last time he had seen Leonardo, he had been giving Alex the big come-on over a glass of high-priced mineral water.

Nice work, Bruce thought resentfully. Leonardo didn't mind ruining Bruce and Lila's love life. But it didn't seem to occur to him that he should curtail his own romantic activities with Alexandra Rollins—who was too young for him, in Bruce's opinion.

Noah Pearson was another guy who'd been perfectly happy until Leonardo had come along. He and Alex had looked like a couple of people who really had a good thing going.

Bruce spotted Leonardo and Alex walking into the café. It looked as if they had just taken a romantic walk around the deck. Leonardo held Alex's hand and was speaking urgently to her as they sat down at their table.

Bruce took a deep breath and composed himself. *I'm Bruce Patman. I'm one of the best-looking guys on the Sweet Valley University campus. And I'm rich. So I'm just going to walk over there and tell him how it's gonna be. If he doesn't like it, he can get off the boat.*

"Excuse me." Bruce tapped Leonardo on the shoulder.

"Hi, Bruce." Alex gave him a smile.

"May I help you with something?" Leonardo asked. His tone wasn't exactly unfriendly, but it certainly wasn't warm.

"I was wondering if you and I could have a little chat. Privately."

Alex quickly reached for her purse. "You guys talk. I'll just go to the—"

Leonardo waved her back into her seat. "No, no," he insisted. "Stay. I will take a short walk with Bruce and be right back." He lifted his hand and gestured to a waiter with an elegant flick of his wrist. Then he pointed to their empty cup and glass, indicating to the waiter that he and Alex would like another round.

Leonardo rose and stood beside his seat, bowing in his quaint, courtly way. "Excuse me, please. I shall be right back."

Bruce and Leonardo walked several yards away until they were out of earshot and out of sight of the café. Leonardo turned to Bruce, his face cold. "Yes?"

67

"I wanted to talk to you about Lila. She's unhappy. *Very* unhappy."

"Yes. I have been thinking about Lila too. I know that she is unhappy. And therefore, she should return with me to Italy and live with her mother-in-law. She needs time to mourn my late brother, and I think she will be happier surrounded by people who knew him and loved him. I will make the arrangements and inform Lila in the morning."

Leonardo started to walk away, but Bruce put a hand on his sleeve and detained him. "You're not reading me, pal."

"Pardon?"

"You're not getting what I'm saying. The reason Lila is unhappy is because she and I can't be together."

Leonardo let out a derisive snort.

"I'm serious. Lila doesn't need to go to Italy with you and sit around some depressing castle with people wearing black and bawling over Tisiano. She needs to go to the beach *with me*. She needs to go dancing *with me*. She needs some romance in her life again—*with me*."

Suddenly Leonardo looked furious. And when he spoke, his accent was thicker and his voice shook with emotion. "My brother, the late count, is hardly cold in his grave. Where I come from, only the lowest *contadino*—peasant—exploits the grief of a young widow in an effort to ingratiate himself."

Leonardo's stare was filled with contempt. He looked as though he wanted to spit in Bruce's face. And he seemed to be getting angrier by the second. "You . . . you . . . If we were in my country," Leonardo said in a menacing tone, shaking his fist.

That did it. Bruce was through being patient. With a quick movement he pulled off his coat. "Okay, pal. You wanna settle this with fists? Let's do it. Let's get it over and done with and then you can get back in your helicopter and—"

"Bruce!" he heard Lila shout. "Leonardo! Stop it!"

Bruce and Leonardo froze as Lila came running toward them in her filmy slip evening dress and high-heeled silver sandals. A gauzy wrap floated around her shoulders like a wisp of smoke in the night breeze. "What are you doing?" she cried. "What's going on here?"

"Lila," Bruce said calmly. "Why don't you go back to your cabin and I'll come explain everything in a few minutes?"

Leonardo grabbed Bruce by the shirtfront. "You will *not* be going to her cabin for *any* reason. Not so long as I am on this boat. As her brother-in-law, I am responsible for her, and I *order* you to stay away—"

"Shut up!" Bruce said, violently shaking off Leonardo's hand and shoving his shoulder.

Leonardo returned Bruce's shove. Seconds later the two men were scuffling on the deck.

"Stop it," Lila shouted, her voice choking with tears. "Please! If either one of you cares at all about me . . ."

The pain in her voice almost brought tears to Bruce's own eyes. But he couldn't stop. He wanted to grab Leonardo by the throat and throw him overboard. How could he not see how perfect Bruce and Lila were together? Why was Leonardo so determined to stand in their way?

Bruce pulled back his fist. He was preparing to deliver a punch when Lila stepped directly in front of his gaze. "Stop it," she was screaming. "Stop it, Bruce. Please."

Breathing heavily, Bruce lowered his fist.

Lila looked from one angry face to the other. "Don't fight. Please. Don't fight." She turned her large blue eyes toward Leonardo. "There's no reason for you to be upset. I'm doing what I can to honor Tisiano's memory. Bruce and I are not seeing each other, and . . . and . . ."

Her lips began to tremble, and she threw a last, agonizing glance at Bruce. ". . . and we never will again."

With a sob she began to run, away from Leonardo and away from Bruce.

"Lila! Wait!" Bruce felt Leonardo's hand on his sleeve, but he tore his arm away and went chasing after her. "I love you!" he shouted behind her, desperately trying to catch up. "Lila, I love you. Doesn't that mean anything at all?"

He caught up with her just as she darted into the door of her luxurious stateroom. His hand shot up and blocked the door before she could slam it shut in his face.

"Please go away," she sobbed, trying to push the door shut.

"No," he said, breathing hard but doing his best to hang on to his dignity. "No, I won't. Not until you tell me that you don't love me. Because if you *really* don't love me, I'll go away."

There was a long pause, and Lila didn't answer. "Forget me," she finally whispered. "It doesn't matter who I love or don't love now. I used to love Tisiano. And now he's dead. And Leonardo is right. Loving you dishonors him."

The door shut quietly. And from inside, Bruce heard the soft click of the lock.

Tom watched Elizabeth walk toward the refreshment table. He quickly looked around. Todd was nowhere to be seen. Maybe he'd gone to the men's room. And for once, Jessica seemed to be otherwise occupied.

He started in Elizabeth's direction. Maybe if they could just talk for a few minutes—alone and uninterrupted—they could get things straightened out.

Elizabeth picked up a cup, and Tom managed to reach her side in time to beat her to the punch ladle. "May I?" he asked.

Elizabeth hesitated a moment, then shrugged. "Why not?"

As Tom filled her glass with punch, he noticed that the pink liquid was almost the exact same color as her lips. "You look beautiful," he couldn't help saying.

He saw her jaw tighten, and she looked away.

"I'm sorry," he said, reaching for a cup for himself. "I didn't mean to say that. I know you probably don't want to hear a lot of compliments from me."

Elizabeth said nothing, but she didn't walk away, either. Tom took that as a good sign. He filled his own glass and cast about desperately for something to say. It seemed as if he'd been waiting endlessly for a chance to speak with her privately. "Elizabeth . . ." he began.

"Yes?" Her tone was bored and resentful. It was the tone a girl would use to get rid of an irritating boor who was bugging her at a party. It was so demoralizing, his mind went even blanker.

"Elizabeth . . ." he repeated weakly.

Her eyes flickered over the crowded ballroom, as if searching for someone to come and rescue her. Somebody like Wilkins.

He opened and closed his mouth a couple of times. There had to be magic words somewhere in the recesses of his brain that would undo the damage he had done.

But before he could find the words, Todd

appeared in the doorway, looked around for Elizabeth, and then started in their direction.

Elizabeth's hand tightened around her cup. If Tom wanted to make up, why didn't he say so? Why didn't he just tell her he loved her and only her and . . .

Todd was getting closer, and Elizabeth felt like bursting into tears. She'd never, ever felt so confused.

On the one hand, she was furious with Tom. She was through with him. He was history.

But on the other hand, she wanted him to turn back into the guy she'd thought he was. She wanted him to say something or do something that would make it okay to love him again.

As soon as she and Tom had broken up, she'd turned to Todd for comfort. It had felt so natural and comfortable to be with him again, she had mistaken her feelings—thinking that she was still in love with him, too.

But she wasn't. And she hadn't told him. And she should tell him. But she couldn't. She felt pretty sure he didn't love her either. But was afraid to tell her. How had everything gotten so tangled?

She drank her punch, almost wishing it were rat poison. This dance felt like the longest dance in her life. And this vacation felt like the longest in the world. She just didn't know how much more fun she could stand.

Todd's eyes hardened when he saw Tom. Beside her, she could feel Tom bristle. If any more unpleasant words were exchanged, she was going to run shrieking to the side of the boat and fling herself overboard.

In an effort to forestall any trouble, she hurried forward and gave Todd the biggest smile she could manage. "Todd!" she cooed in a melodious tone. "Did you find Jess?"

Todd shook his head. "Nope. No sign of her anywhere." He threw a dirty look at Tom and put an arm protectively around Elizabeth's shoulders. "Don't worry. Jessica's like a cat. She always lands on her feet. And if I know your twin, she's somewhere flirting. So let's quit worrying and enjoy the dance."

Elizabeth let him lead her back to the dance floor and put her arms around his neck to dance. *Quit worrying.* That's what everyone kept telling her to do. But it was easier said than done. Especially when she was worried about Jessica.

The itsy-bitsy spider climbed up the waterspout.
Jessica hummed the children's song tunelessly as
she stared dully at the little spider crawling up the
dilapidated and rusty water pipe that ran from the
little sink, up the wall, and across the ceiling.

Usually Jessica hated spiders with a passion.
But singing about spiders somehow made them
easier to tolerate. And it was getting pretty lonely
in this cell. She wasn't going to turn up her nose
at company, even if it did have eight legs.

She was bored. No. She was too nervous to be
bored. But she was nervous and worn out with
waiting. It seemed as if she had been sitting in the
little jail cell for hours. All pleas to allow her to
make a phone call or contact the ship had been
met with the same response: "Just wait for your
lawyer."

"When is he getting here?" she had asked over and

over. Their only response was a disinterested shrug.

She checked her watch and felt her heart drop. The boat was still at the dock. But it would be leaving soon. Nobody knew she'd been taken into custody. The authorities weren't allowing her to contact anybody. If the boat left, she would be one more missing person. Another name on the list headed by Winston Egbert and Denise Waters.

She walked over to the bars, grabbed them, and began to shake. "Hey!" she yelled. "Don't I get anything to eat?"

From the outer room she heard the police captain respond, "You will eat when your lawyer gets here."

She walked over to the filthy bed with the threadbare, sheetless mattress and sat down on the edge of it. No way would she lie on it. It looked like a guaranteed fleabag.

Jessica heard the front door open and close with a bang. "I'd like to see the police captain," said a deep, authoritative voice. "Now!"

It was as if a bolt of electricity had come bursting through the door. The whole atmosphere inside the jail changed.

"I am the police captain," Captain Jay said, his voice sounding a bit flustered. "Who are you?"

The listless guard who had been snoozing in a folding chair at the end of the corridor stood up, straightened his uniform, and marched around the corner into the lobby.

Jessica got up and moved to the door of the cell, pricking up her ears so she could hear every word.

"I understand you're holding a Ms. Jessica Wakefield," the man said in a tone of profound disapproval.

"Yes, that is correct."

There was a long pause.

"I do not think you can possibly be aware of the gravity of this situation," the deep voice went on to say.

"Gravity of what situation? The young lady is a pickpocket and a thief. What is your interest in the matter?"

"I am vice consul for the U.S. Caribbean Consul Delegation on Trade, Human Rights, and Maritime Law. And I am shocked, deeply shocked, to discover that you are holding Ms. Wakefield. Are you aware that she is a U.S. citizen and a student?"

"Yes, but . . ."

"Are you aware that you are in violation of subsection B of International Code TR8709524 in the newly instated Articles of Maritime International Legal Procedures in regard to the arrest and questioning of students on foreign soil? Violation of these codes is considered a very serious breach, not only of law but of carefully cultivated diplomatic ties. I wouldn't be at all surprised if this incident were to be construed as an act of war!"

Jessica pressed her face against the bars of her cell, listening to the men converse around the corner. She had expected a laid-back island attorney in Bermuda shorts. But the guy out there sounded as if he'd come right from the upper echelon of the State Department.

"Act of war!" the police captain cried. "We had no such intention. You are quite mistaken. We have not been informed about such a subsection or International Code number. . . ." He trailed off helplessly.

"Ignorance of the law is no excuse. I'm late for a meeting now with the U.S. ambassador and her husband. But I have one piece of advice. If you wish to avoid an international incident, release that young woman and release her *now*. Good night."

Jessica's eyes were wide and her heart was racing. Would they let her go?

Within seconds, the police captain was hurrying around the corner with a large bundle of keys in his hand. "A million apologies, Ms. Wakefield," he said quickly. "We seem to have made a mistake. You are free to go."

Jessica stepped out of the jail cell, half convinced she was dreaming. "Who was that man?" she asked.

"The vice president of something," the police captain said, clearly intimidated. "Frankly, I am not sure. But we do not . . . *do not* want any kind of international incident with the United States. Therefore, I am allowing you to return to your ship. I urge you to hurry."

Jessica checked her watch. "Wow. I'd better get going."

The police captain ushered her to the door, and the two policemen sprang to open it for her as if she were a millionairess leaving the Plaza Hotel.

As soon as Jessica was out the door she broke into a run, determined to catch up with the lawyer and thank him.

The path that led away from the rustic police station was dark and paved with oyster shells. Up ahead she could hear his footsteps crunching on the shells. She could barely make out the lines of a dark silhouette as he disappeared in the distance, taking long strides.

"Hey," she cried.

The pace of the crunching accelerated.

"Sir! Wait, please!" She quickened her own step, listening to the shells crunch beneath her low-heeled evening pumps. "Wait. I want to thank you!"

The man ahead of her veered off the path and began to jog, moving as quickly away as possible.

How weird, Jessica thought. *It's like he's trying to avoid me.*

He stumbled slightly, and she heard him let out a little snort of anger. Very quickly he removed his shoe, shook out a shell, and replaced it.

He turned a little toward Jessica, who was rapidly gaining on him. Then she skidded to complete stop, amazed. Her *lawyer* was tall and broad shouldered, with a head of very dark hair. He wore a blue blazer and tie and he looked very adult. Very much like a U.S. vice consul acting on behalf of an embassy.

But he wasn't. He was her guardian angel. And he'd just sprung her from jail by means of a clever scam. Jessica's heart swelled. She lifted her arms. "Wait!" she cried in a throbbing voice. "Please don't run away. Please."

Her angel took off running, disappearing so deeply into the dark night that she could no longer even hear his footsteps. She was afraid to follow. The *Homecoming Queen* was leaving soon and she didn't want to get left on this island.

It wouldn't be long before the local police discovered that they had been tricked. If they got their hands on her again, they might lock her up and throw away the key.

Jessica turned in the direction of the boat and began running, hoping that her guardian angel was following her at a safe distance. She didn't want him getting marooned on this island either.

There was a soft knock on the door. Lila hesitated for a moment before opening it. She had been crying ever since she returned to her cabin, and she knew she looked awful.

If it was Bruce, she didn't want him to see her

looking this way. For that matter, she didn't want anybody to see her looking this way.

"Lila!" she heard Leonardo's voice call out from the other side of the paneled door. "It is your brother-in-law. May I speak with you, please?"

Lila opened the door. As soon as Leonardo saw her face, he frowned deeply. "Lila! My poor little sister-in-law." He put his arms around her in a brotherly fashion and walked her over to the large, overstuffed armchair.

Then he knelt, taking both her hands in his. He stared at her with large and sympathetic eyes. "You are very sad, yes?"

Lila nodded. Yes. She was. And as awful as she looked, she was glad for him to see how unhappy she was.

"It is normal. Very natural. When one is deeply in love, it is hard to be apart."

Lila's heart lifted. It sounded as if he had thought things over and reconsidered his position. "Yes. Yes. It's so hard to be apart," she agreed in a choking voice.

"It's not right that you be alone. Solitude gives a young woman too much time to think and grow sad."

"That's right." Lila gulped. "And I feel as if I've been alone so much that—"

"Do not worry," he said in a kind voice. "Leonardo has a plan to take care of everything."

"A plan?"

He nodded. "Yes. I have a duty to look after you. To see to your happiness. That's what Tisiano would have wanted. And I know, as his brother, that he would have wanted me to take you back to Italy to live with our mother. She lives very quietly in the country with her two sisters—my maiden aunts—Theresa and Maria." He kissed his fingers in tribute. "They are so beautiful. So kind. They are like saints."

Lila felt her heart stick in her chest. What a horrible plan.

"And they will be so happy to have you. They have so little company, it will be good for all of you. Alessandra and I will come and see you now and then. Drop in and bring you news."

He stood and beamed at her. "It is beautiful in the country. You will love it there. So peaceful. So . . . how you say . . . *healing*." His face darkened. "You will heal and be strong and not so vulnerable to . . . *predators* like Bruce Patman."

Lila stared at him, bereft of speech.

"So," he said briskly, leaning over to kiss Lila's cheek. "You go to bed. Get a good night of beauty sleep. And tomorrow I will call and make all the arrangements. *Bona notte*." Leonardo slipped out the door and closed it quietly behind him.

Lila sat staring at the door, holding her breath. Then she bent forward until her forehead touched her knees and wept.

Chapter Seven

"He's telling him. I just know he's telling him," Nicole said for about the fiftieth time in her teary whisper.

"Shhh," Tom said, his voice soothing. "Stay cool. We don't know what they're talking about."

"They're talking about us," Nicole whimpered, wringing her hands.

"Stop doing that. It makes you look guilty." His tone was a little sharper than he'd intended it to be. But Nicole's nerves were beginning to get on Tom's nerves, and it took all his self-control not to snap.

Two minutes ago, Danny had entered the ballroom looking like a man about to deliver a subpoena. He'd tapped Jason on the shoulder and asked if he could speak to him privately. Then he'd led him out of the ballroom and into a secluded corner of the outdoor pavilion.

Tom and Nicole could see them talking from where they stood. And they watched with a growing sense of dread.

"He'll cancel the wedding," Nicole whispered. "I know he will."

"Well," Tom said out of the side of his mouth and smiling cordially at a guy he recognized from his chemistry class. "Maybe that wouldn't be the worst thing that could happen. Look at how all this started. Jason was busy hanging out with his guy friends and it hurt your feelings. Maybe he's not ready to get married. And maybe you aren't either."

"Who cares?" she squeaked. "If we don't get married, I'll look like a huge idiot. I've got ten bridesmaids. *Ten*. And fifty friends onboard for this wedding. I've been planning it for weeks." She sighed. "I've written to every single friend and relative I have and told them I'm getting married. I'd rather die than leave this ship single," she finished dramatically.

Tom took a deep breath and tried to find the humor in the situation. "Nicole," he said calmly. "You don't get married because you've booked the bridesmaids. You get married because you're in love."

In love the way I'm in love with Elizabeth.

And the way he wished she were in love with him.

But Nicole wasn't in any mood to listen, and her

panicky voice droned on and on, outlining one disastrous scenario after the other. Jason would kill her. Jason would kill Tom. Jason would kill himself. Jason would kill her. Kill Tom. Then kill himself.

There was more along the same lines, but Tom tuned it out. Jason wasn't the type of guy who'd kill anybody. He was good-natured and trusting. The worst thing that would happen was that there would be some ugly scenes, some harsh words, and everybody would look bad and be embarrassed.

Tom wished she would just be quiet for a while so he could think about Elizabeth. He needed to come up with a plan that would get her back.

Elizabeth had been profoundly hurt and betrayed. He couldn't blame her for hating him. But he had to figure out some way to make her understand that it wasn't as bad as it looked.

And he had to make Danny forgive him. Danny had looked just as angry and betrayed as Elizabeth. He couldn't be madder if it had been Isabella he'd caught Tom kissing.

But Danny was Danny. And since Nicole was Jason's fiancée, in Danny's mind what Tom had done was as bad as cheating with a married woman.

"I'll never live it down if I get jilted. Never."

"Please get a grip, Nicole," Tom begged. "We don't know what they're talking about. Danny is Jason's best man. They might be making some kind of last-minute arrangements about the wedding."

Nicole took some deep breaths and her face broke into a grimacing smile as she waved and nodded at two of her friends wafting by in silky dresses. "Maybe. But if Jason finds out, there's no telling what he'll do. Sometimes he really flies off the handle."

"He won't find out," Tom said, sending up a silent prayer. *I hope.*

Nicole moaned, as if a new and horrible thought had just occurred to her. "What if he gets off the boat like that guy Bryan did and leaves me here to cope with all these people?" she asked in a voice thick with tears. "What if he just throws his stuff in a suitcase and goes?"

Just as she said that, Nina Harper twirled by, dancing with Dr. Daniels. "Boy," Nicole said, sounding a little resentful. "Nina sure came out of that fiasco looking good. Her boyfriend walked off the boat and left her—but it didn't take her more than a couple of hours to line up somebody else. And she traded up, too. The guy's a doctor and way better looking than Bryan."

Tom grunted his agreement, but he didn't altogether approve of Nina and Dr. Daniels. Nina had been flirting with the doctor ever since the ship left Miami. No wonder Bryan had split.

But it was none of his business, and he didn't want to fall into the Danny trap—getting involved in other people's business and making all kinds of judgments.

He heard Nina laughing as she twirled around. Her bright red skirt flew up to reveal her shapely, well-muscled legs.

Nina was athletic, and she was as at ease on the dance floor as she was in a swimming pool or on a tennis court. She wasn't thin and willowy like Elizabeth. But she had a great figure, and she had those really sexy good looks that went with being healthy and happy about oneself.

Self-confidence was an attractive feature, Tom reflected. It was what had attracted him to Elizabeth. And it was Nicole's lack of it that was turning him off right now.

She was still going on and on about how afraid she was of looking silly. He wished he could just tell her to shut up. But the last thing he needed was for her to get even more upset and have a complete breakdown.

A bead of sweat began creeping down Tom's temple. He couldn't help wondering whether he'd wind up with one enemy on the boat, or several. Right now Danny seemed determined to cut him out of his life forever. If Jason found out—and so did his friends—this ship was going to be very unpleasant for Tom.

"What about Elizabeth?" Nicole hissed. "Even if Danny doesn't say anything to Jason, don't you think she'll tell him to get even with me?"

Tom turned. "That's not the kind of thing Elizabeth would do," he said angrily. "Elizabeth

87

doesn't *get even* with people. She's a grown-up. And no matter how angry she is with me, she'd never do anything to hurt you."

"Sorry," Nicole said in a subdued voice.

When Tom looked into the large, unhappy eyes of his old high school girlfriend, he felt some of his irritation with her slip away.

He was responsible for a lot of her trouble; the least he could do for her was be supportive. He put his hand on Nicole's arm and squeezed it. "I don't think Danny will tell Jason he saw us kissing. He'll want to," he added quickly. "In his ethical system, that's the right thing to do. But I think Isabella's pretty adamant that he mind his own business, and Danny can usually be trusted to do what Isabella says."

Nicole's eyes followed Nina's progress across the dance floor. "What was I thinking?" she said mournfully. "How did I let this happen? Why on earth did I throw myself at you like that?"

"Hey! You didn't throw yourself at me. Stop beating up on yourself. And you weren't thinking. You were feeling. You were feeling all the same things I was feeling. We felt abandoned. And we felt alone." He held one of her soft hands in his. With his other hand, he stroked the outside of her arm. "Under the circumstances, it seemed natural to turn to each other and . . ."

*   *   *

"Having a good time?" Nina asked Elizabeth as she and Dr. Daniels spun to a stop and took a break.

Elizabeth gave Nina a tight smile. "I'm having a great time. A really great time." Out of the corner of her eye, she saw Tom standing with Nicole—stroking her arm.

Honestly! How low was Tom Watts prepared to sink?

Minutes after he'd tried to cozy up to Elizabeth, he was hanging around Nicole again, looking down at her doe eyes while fondling her arm. It made Elizabeth so angry she felt like running over there and kicking him. But no way would she give him the satisfaction.

"We're having a wonderful time. Right, Todd?" she repeated in a voice she hoped was loud enough to be overheard.

Todd seemed distracted and didn't answer. He sipped his punch and stared at the dancers with a distracted frown.

Elizabeth saw Tom's eyes flicker in their direction. Determined to make sure he knew she didn't care about him, she threw back her head and let out what she hoped was an infectious, silvery laugh.

Much to her irritation, Todd didn't respond with a chuckling laugh of his own. He jumped a little and gave her a surprised and slightly annoyed look. Maybe her laugh had sounded more tinny than silvery.

89

"I'm having a wonderful time too," Nina said. She laughed, producing a forced cackling noise that didn't sound any more silvery or infectious than Elizabeth's.

Still, Elizabeth grinned and laughed some more.

Dr. Daniels filled their corner with a booming masculine laugh that was so loud, Elizabeth swayed a little and stepped on Todd's toe.

"Oh . . . ha ha." She giggled. "I guess I've had a little too much of this sugary punch."

Tom and Nicole both looked over in their direction, as did almost a third of the ballroom. Elizabeth forced herself to keep smiling.

If Tom Watts thought he had any power to make her unhappy, he was a crazy. At least, that's what she wanted *him* to believe.

"Looks like Elizabeth's having a good time," Nicole commented.

"Looks like it," Tom agreed unhappily.

"Uh-oh." Nicole groaned. "Here they come."

Tom looked up and saw Jason and Danny leave the pavilion and reenter the ballroom. Then Danny hurried out a side door and Jason continued across the ballroom in Tom and Nicole's direction.

Tom felt his face turn beet red when he realized that he was holding Nicole's arm. He abruptly released it. "We're just destined to be misunderstood. It's like a farce. Only, I don't hear anybody laughing. We exchange a couple of little bitty kisses—and now nobody will speak to me."

"Little bitty kisses?" Nicole repeated faintly, lifting her fingers to straighten her hair.

Tom's heart sank even further. It was pretty obvious that now he'd even offended Nicole. "Big kisses," he amended quickly. "Great kisses. In fact, they practically knocked me off my feet."

But Nicole was too anxious to pay attention. Jason was getting closer, and Tom felt Nicole move slightly behind him, as if for protection. "He knows," she said. "I might as well just jump over the side now. I can tell he knows. Look at his face."

Tom drew his hand down over his own face, stretching the skin and trying to relax all the thousands of tight, tense muscles around his brow and jaw.

A matter of a few feet separated them now. But Jason's face was blank.

Tom moved a little closer to Nicole. She wasn't his girlfriend. But if Jason made any kind of scene, he was prepared to get her out of there before Jason could say anything too wounding.

They were face to face now. Practically nose to nose. "Tom. Nicole," Jason said sharply. "We need to talk."

Chapter
Eight

Lila lay on her bed, exhausted from crying. In her hand, she clutched her favorite picture of Tisiano. It was surrounded by an ornate, sterling silver frame with blue velvet backing.

She was sentimental about the picture for two reasons. It contained a picture of Tisiano, a man she had loved very much. And the frame had been a wedding present from Jessica.

She carried the picture with her always, as she had when she was married to Tisiano. He had traveled a lot on business. When he had been away, she'd had the photograph to keep her company. The picture somehow managed to capture all of his charm and humor.

And when she had been living in Italy and feeling homesick for Sweet Valley, she had enjoyed stroking the complex lines of the frame and thinking about Jessica. And about how their lives had gone from simple to complex in such a short time.

High school had been so uncomplicated. Basically it had consisted of dates, arguments, homework, and parties. It was a lot different from being an adult and marrying into one of the oldest and richest families in Europe.

Her marriage had been a short, brief love affair with a storybook prince. But he had died in a Jet Ski accident. And the prince was gone now. Forever.

Soon after Tisiano's funeral she had returned to Sweet Valley University, enrolled in classes, and tried to pick up her life where she had left off. It had been hard, but Bruce had made it easier. They seemed to complement each other in a unique way.

They were both rich. They had both grown up having everything they wanted. Little by little, though, their two selfish natures were beginning to become a little less self-centered. They were learning to compromise. To care about each other instead of only about themselves.

Lila lay on her back and felt the tears trickle from the outer corner of her eye and roll down her temple. The beautiful blue-and-white molding on the ceiling blurred.

She had almost begun to believe that she was one of those rare and blessed people who actually found true love twice in one life. After Tisiano died, Bruce had stepped in and filled up all the empty spaces in her heart. He had dulled the pain of her grief by keeping her giggling at his foolish jokes. And at night, he took her in his strong arms and drove all memories of Tisiano away.

She glanced at the photo. Was it her imagination, or was Tisiano's image frowning? Lila put the picture facedown on the bed, unable to look at it anymore.

Even if her late husband wasn't frowning, Leonardo certainly was. He made her feel cheap and gauche and unworthy of the love of such a great man.

She turned the picture faceup again. "What would you want me to do?" she asked out loud, wishing Tisiano's spirit could be present in the room to answer her. "Do you really want me to bury myself alive?"

But there was no sound beyond the loud ticking of the clock over the bed.

Lila closed her eyes. Maybe she could determine what Tisiano would want for her if she could imagine what she would want for him if their positions were reversed.

Lila took two deep breaths, preparing herself for what was going to be a difficult mental exercise. She closed her eyes and pictured herself racing across the Mediterranean Sea on a Jet Ski, then disappearing in a column of flame and a shower of sparks.

She saw Tisiano on the patio of their villa,

watching helplessly while the wreckage from the accident drifted away.

A series of montages played in her mind. Her funeral. Tisiano in a black suit placing a rose on her casket. His hundreds of relatives in their black dresses and lace head coverings. A line of long black limos moving through the drizzly gray afternoon. Handkerchiefs. Umbrellas. Tears.

Then, afterward, she saw Tisiano thin and haggard. She imagined him taking time away from the office and refusing to see friends.

Finally someone would coax him out of the house and convince him to resume some of his old activities. It would be someone nonthreatening or familiar. Someone who had known her. Elizabeth. Or Jessica. Or Alex.

Lila's mind raced ahead, picturing Tisiano and Jessica on picnics. Visiting museums. And dining in elegant restaurants.

At first, they would talk only about how much they missed her. Jessica would tell him all about the childhoods they had shared. And Tisiano would reminisce at great length about all of Lila's endearing qualities.

They would trade anecdotes and laugh. And then trade more anecdotes and cry, hugging each other for comfort. Then one day, inevitably, the hug would last just a few moments longer than it had the day before. They would look at each other . . .

"Ohhhhh," Lila moaned, picturing Tisiano in Jessica's arms. The pain of seeing Tisiano with someone else was so great she rolled off the bed and curled into a ball on the carpeted floor. "No!" she wept. "No! No! No!"

Leonardo was absolutely right, she realized. It was too soon.

Bruce kept reminding her that Tisiano was gone. Bruce was right, but Lila still wasn't ready to let go of him. She wasn't.

She grabbed the photograph of Tisiano off the bed and hugged it possessively against her chest.

Jason shook his head sadly. "Nicole, honey. I'm afraid the wedding's off."

Nicole sucked in her breath so loudly that Tom thought she might be about to faint. He felt his stomach begin to churn with dread.

"Oh, Jason," she wailed. "Please don't do this to me. Please."

Jason took both her hands in his, looking her in the eye. Disappointment was written all over his face. "Nicole, I think you know that I have pretty strong feelings on some subjects."

"But Jason . . ." she protested.

He held up a hand, stemming the flow of her words. "I know you think I'm old-fashioned, but—"

"Nobody is *that* old-fashioned," she cried,

becoming increasingly agitated. "Jason. I want to get married. I want to marry you." Her voice rose an octave. "I've got ten bridesmaids on this ship and—"

"But we don't have a ring!" Jason shouted, releasing her hands and waving his arms in the air. "My mom's ring. It's gone. Somebody stole it from Danny's room. We hoped we'd find it before we had to tell anybody, but—"

"The ring is gone?" she repeated.

Jason nodded. "That's right. No wedding ring, Nicole. You don't want to get married without a ring, do you?"

Nicole's color began to return to normal. "You're telling me the reason we can't get married is because you don't have the ring?"

"That's right." He nodded slowly.

"He doesn't have the ring," Nicole said to Tom, almost laughing. "Oh, Jason." She threw her arms around his neck. "Who cares about a ring when we have each other?"

"I do," he insisted, removing her arms. "That wedding ring has come down through four generations of Pierce women. In my family, it's bad luck to get married without it."

Nicole's expression turned from anxious to stormy in less than five seconds. The look on her face was so ominous, Tom's protective instincts shifted from Nicole to Jason.

Nicole was pretty volatile and right now, with

her hands on her hips and her eyes snapping, she looked dangerous. "Jason Pierce. You're just using that ring as an excuse."

"An excuse?" he exclaimed. "An excuse for what?"

"An excuse to cancel the wedding because you don't really want to get married."

"I do too!"

"No, you don't. You'd rather spend the rest of your life hanging around with your buddies than get married."

"No, I wouldn't."

"Yes, you would. You're just not man enough to admit it. So instead of being honest, you're handing me some lame story about a missing wedding ring."

"Nicole. You've got it all wrong."

Tom edged away. Nicole's voice was getting louder, and the little group was attracting a lot of attention.

"Well, you listen to me, Jason Pierce. You can just go ahead and hang around with your precious friends for the rest of your life if you want to. I'm getting off this boat right now and *you* can deal with the ten bridesmaids, the ten groomsmen, and the fifty guests."

She turned and began to flounce away. But Jason caught her by the hand, pulled her into his embrace, and planted a passionate kiss on her pouting lips. "All right. All right," he said a few moments later. "You win. Forget the ring. We'll get married tomorrow and worry about the bad luck later."

Nicole smiled like a Cheshire cat. "You're sure?"

"I'm sure. In fact, I'm so sure, I want to do this thing with the biggest-possible amount of splash."

Jason hurried toward the bandstand. He exchanged a few quick words with the lead singer, who turned and signaled the band. The music ceased, bringing the dancing to an abrupt halt. A curious buzz filled the room as the lead singer handed Jason his microphone.

"Fellow collegians and cruisers," Jason began, drawing laughter from the crowd. "I'm sorry to interrupt your dance, but I want to make an announcement. Ms. Nicole Riley and I will be married here in this ballroom tomorrow morning at eleven A.M."

He paused and gave everyone an opportunity to applaud. When the clapping died down, he smiled. "Nicole and I would like to extend an invitation to each and every person onboard this ship to be our guest for the ceremony and the reception."

He handed the microphone back to the lead singer as the crowd enthusiastically whistled and stamped their feet.

"Happy?" Tom asked Nicole out of the side of his mouth.

"I'd be happier if we could tie Danny Wyatt up and keep him locked in a closet until after the reception tomorrow," she shot back. "I feel like we've got a loose cannon rolling around on deck. And it's only a matter of time before it goes off and hurts somebody."

Chapter Nine

Jessica approached the dock with her shoes in her hand. She had jogged barefoot almost all the way from the jail. It had been impossible to run in her evening pumps.

She could hear music, and up on deck she could see couples dancing. Jessica glanced cautiously around before setting foot on the brightly lit pier. By now the police had probably realized that she had escaped the island jail illegally. And they were most likely on their way to apprehend her again.

Jessica's plan was to get to her cabin, change into something nondescript, and hide her hair under a baseball cap. Then she would complete her search for her mystery man while the dance was in progress.

She darted across the pier and tiptoed up the entrance to the ship. Luckily she was able to board unseen, and she began hurrying toward the corridor that led to her cabin.

The lights were dim in the main hall, and the cabins seemed to be pretty deserted. Most people were either at the dance or in one of the clubs.

So far, so good. She was almost home free. But just as she turned the last corner, she let out a little shriek and her hand flew to her mouth. She was standing face to face with none other than Federico Esteban, the steward who had accused her of stealing Jason's ring.

Federico looked as surprised to see her as she was to see him. And his little pencil mustache quivered with indignation and distaste.

Jessica's fear gave way to anger. "Listen," she said. "Don't give me that look. I'm not too crazy about you, either. And take my advice. Don't mess with Jessica Wakefield!"

He drew himself up, still staring at her wordlessly. Then he opened his mouth wide. "Thief!" he shouted at the top of his lungs. "Thief!"

"I am not!" Jessica insisted. "Shut up!"

But Federico was shouting too loudly to hear her protests. "Thief!" he cried. He hurried to the intercom phone that was mounted on the wall and picked it up. "Deck five," he barked. "Send security." Then he banged down the receiver.

Jessica dropped her shoes, backed up, and took off down the carpeted hallway, going as fast as she could.

But Federico was quick. And she could tell by the thumping sound of his shoes on the carpet that he was getting closer to her.

It was a long hallway, with several interconnecting corridors. Jessica wondered if she should hook a hard left into one of the hallways. Unfortunately she couldn't remember which ones were dead ends. The last thing she needed was to get cornered.

After jogging over dirt roads and oyster shell paths, her feet were blistered and aching. She was losing speed.

At the end of the corridor was a stairwell. If she could just get to that stairwell, maybe she could lose him on the next deck.

Jessica thought she could feel his breath on the back of her neck, he was getting so close. "Oh no," she wailed. "I don't want to go back to that jail."

A large foot protruded from around a corner.

Jessica gracefully leapt over it. But behind her, the steward wasn't as lucky. She heard him let out a yell of surprise and then a grunt of pain when he hit the floor with a loud thump.

Jessica didn't stop long enough to admire her guardian angel's handiwork or say thanks. But it was nice to know he was back onboard—and back on the job.

She jerked open the door of the stairwell and raced up two flights. Then she paused and pressed her ear against the door she'd reached. She heard nothing on the other side, so she cautiously opened the door and peeked out.

It was the entertainment deck, where the bowling alley, video arcade, and movie theater were. Because of the dance, the place was deserted.

She saw the usher at the entrance of the movie theater yawn. Then he ambled over to a closet, removed a small broom and dustpan, and began sweeping up some popcorn that had spilled in front of the refreshment counter.

Very quietly, Jessica tiptoed past him and into the dark of the movie theater. It would be a perfect place to hide. Pretty soon this boat was going to be crawling with police. But they wouldn't find her. And since the ship was due to sail, eventually they'd have to disembark—without Jessica.

Gin-Yung listened to the rustle of her dress as she and Noah danced. The subtle sound was kind of unnerving. She wasn't used to clothes that made noise.

But then again, the saleslady in the shop had made a big deal about the material being taffeta. Maybe all taffeta dresses crackled. "Noah, do you know anything about taffeta?" she asked as they walked off the dance floor when the song was over.

Noah scratched his head, looking bewildered. "Taffeta . . . hmmm. There are so many personality disorders, it's hard to keep them all straight. Let's see now, is it a phobia or a mania?"

"It's not a personality disorder. It's a fabric."

"Oh. No. I'm sorry. I don't know anything about fabric or women's clothes or anything like that."

"Unfortunately I don't either," Gin-Yung said glumly. She caught a glimpse of herself in the mirrored wall and felt her cheeks flush. In spite of the saleslady's hurried alterations, the dress looked awfully big. She looked as if she'd been eaten by a big strawberry pastry. "Do I look as silly as I feel?"

Noah frowned. "Why don't you ask Leonardo? He's the big expert on women's fashion."

"Ha ha," Gin-Yung said dryly. "I'm in pain here, Pearson. If you're so sensitive, how come you're not getting that?"

Noah gave her a kind smile. "I'm sorry. I guess I'm in a very self-involved phase. I was feeling sorry for myself."

Gin-Yung's gaze followed Elizabeth and Todd's progress across the dance floor and she felt Noah flick something from her bare arm.

"Mosquito?" she inquired.

"Heart," he responded. "You're doing what you told me not to do. Wearing your heart on your sleeve."

Gin-Yung rubbed her hands up and down her bare arms. "Speaking of sleeves, I wish I had some. I don't know how girls survive in these dresses. I feel like I'm getting pneumonia."

Noah laughed and put his arms around her. "I think this is the secret." He rubbed his hands up and down her arms.

Both she and Noah began to laugh.

Their laughter caught Todd's attention and he looked over in their direction. She saw him do a double take when he realized that it was she in the pink pouf dress. Gin-Yung snuggled close to Noah and laughed even louder. *This is more like it,* she thought with a glimmer of satisfaction.

"Did you ask them to keep playing this?" Elizabeth said with a soft smile when the band played "Old Times" for what seemed like the fifth time.

"Hmmm?" Todd was watching Noah and Gin-Yung.

"I said, did you ask them to keep playing this?" Her voice sounded slightly irritated at having to repeat the question.

Todd shook his head. "Actually, no. But I guess this song was meaningful to lots of people our age. I'll bet half the couples here think it's their song and requested it."

That wasn't a very loverly response, he realized. And Elizabeth deserved better. He tried to smile as he added a rider. "But I may have mentioned once or twice that we particularly enjoyed hearing it." *Though I don't particularly enjoy watching Noah Pearson paw Gin-Yung to the tune.*

*   *   *

Alex's eyes widened a little as she peered at Noah over Leonardo's shoulder. He was running his hands up and down Gin-Yung's bare arms and laughing in a way he'd never laughed with her.

In fact, Alex couldn't remember Noah's ever being that affectionate. Noah didn't want her. He wanted Gin-Yung. And he probably had from the moment they'd gotten on the ship. Maybe he'd even known her before and had a crush on her. That would explain why he had been so distant and remote.

Her eyelids fluttered closed and she tried hard to block the pain. Clearly Noah was capable of laughter and affection, and maybe even passion—but not with her.

Leonardo's arm pulled her closer to him, and one hand caressed her thick curls. *Take the prince and quit thinking about the frog,* she admonished herself, swallowing hard. *Because the frog doesn't give a ribbit about Alexandra Rollins, and the prince does.*

Elizabeth put her arm through Todd's and leaned against him. His body felt warm and familiar, and it made her ache in a bittersweet way.

She wished Todd's arms could make her feel the way they used to. She wished Todd's kisses could make her forget Tom's.

But they couldn't. If anything, they just made

107

her more painfully aware she was losing something that had meant so much to her.

She swallowed hard, determined not to spend the whole evening weeping into Todd's jacket.

Todd seemed suddenly to notice her emotional state. "It'll be okay, Liz," he promised. He pulled her against him and laid his cheek on top of her head. "Everything is going to work out fine." The words were comforting, but his voice lacked conviction. He sounded tired and discouraged.

"I'm so disillusioned."

Todd sighed. "I wish there were some way to get through life with all of our illusions intact, but there doesn't seem to be. Very few of us are what we seem. For all I know, you may be the only one who truly is as honest and caring and loving on the inside as you are on the outside."

Suddenly, from out of nowhere, two policemen appeared at their sides. Each one put a hand on Elizabeth's arm and pulled her out of Todd's embrace. "You are under arrest, Ms. Wakefield."

"Who the . . ." Todd started forward but was shoved roughly backward by one of the policemen.

Elizabeth's mouth opened and closed in shock until she was finally able to squeak, "What am I under arrest for?"

"For stealing a very valuable ring. A ring belonging to Mr. Jason Pierce."

"I didn't steal any ring!"

"That will be for your attorney to prove," the policeman said. "Your *real* attorney. We will not fall for the same trick twice."

"What trick?" Todd demanded, starting forward again. "Who are you people? Take your hands off her."

"Take your hands off her now," Tom Watts ordered, appearing on the scene.

Todd turned. "I'll handle this," he said curtly to Tom. He put his hand on Elizabeth's arm and the policeman shoved him roughly away again.

Tom gave him a contemptuous look. "Doesn't look to me like you're handling anything." He put his hand on Elizabeth's arm and the policeman shoved him in the same direction—where he collided with Todd.

"Get out of the way," Todd yelled.

"You get out of the way," Tom retorted.

"Both of you get out of our way," one of the policemen ordered. "This young lady is going to jail."

"What's going on here?" an authoritative voice demanded. The crowd parted and the captain appeared.

Suddenly everybody in the ballroom was talking at once.

"HOLD IT!" a voice shouted, rising an octave above the others. "NOBODY MOVE!"

The room fell silent and all eyes turned toward Isabella, who stood with her hands on her hips, looking just furious. "I think I can clear this up. Would everyone remain here for a minute, please?"

She held up her hands like a policeman. "Stop! Stay. Don't go away. I'll be right back." And with that, Isabella lifted her skirts and sprinted out of the ballroom.

Isabella flew down the hallway, found Danny's door, and began pounding on it. "Danny Wyatt, you come out of there right now!" she shouted.

The door opened and Danny peered out.

"You didn't tell Jason about the ring, did you?" she accused in a hissing tone.

"I tried to, Isabella. Really."

"But you didn't, did you?"

Danny dropped his eyes and shuffled his feet a little. "No," he muttered like a child caught in a fib. "I tried, but then . . . then he started going on and on about how I was his oldest friend and how he trusted me more than anybody else in the world and . . . what can I say? I just couldn't do it. I didn't have the guts."

"Well, you'd better find the guts and come with me to the ballroom right now. Because two policemen from the island are here to arrest Elizabeth for the *theft of Mr. Pierce's very valuable ring*."

Danny's eyes widened with shock. "Arrest Elizabeth! That's ridiculous. How did that happen?"

"Who knows? Who *cares*? I'm sure we'll find out later. But in the meantime, you'd better get up there with the ring before they haul Elizabeth off the ship and we never see her again for the rest of the cruise."

Danny flew into his cabin, dove toward the mattress, and felt around underneath it until he located the ring. Then he stuck it into the pocket of his dinner jacket. "Okay. Let's go."

"Didn't I tell you not to interfere?" Isabella couldn't help snapping as they started down the corridor.

The policeman stared at the opulent ring that sat in the palm of Danny's hand. They looked at the ring. They looked at Danny. They looked at Jason. They looked at Elizabeth.

Then they looked at each other again.

And they didn't look too happy.

"Would somebody care to give us an explanation, please?" Policeman One said.

"Yeah," Jason said slowly, giving Danny a strange look. "I wouldn't mind getting an explanation myself."

"Me either," Nicole announced, crossing her arms over her chest.

Danny caught a glimpse of himself in the mirror on the wall of the anteroom of the ballroom. He'd never looked so discomfited in his life. "Well," he began uneasily. "It's sort of hard to explain."

"You thought perhaps you could sell the ring at one of the ports," a policeman suggested.

That shocked Danny into a response. "No!" he barked. "I never had any such intention. I'm not a thief."

The policeman stared pointedly at Isabella. "It's a very lovely ring. Perhaps you planned to give it to someone."

"I didn't steal it to sell or to give to someone," Danny explained. "I *borrowed* it. Hid it, really."

"Why?" the policeman asked.

Danny swallowed. "To . . . to . . . well . . . it's like this. I, uh . . . I knew that Jason wouldn't want to get married without the ring. And I also thought he and Nicole needed more time to think about what they were doing. So I figured if I hid the ring for a while, it would force them to take a little bit more time over this decision."

"And what, exactly, made you think that Nicole and I needed more time to think it over?" Jason asked slowly.

Tom's ears felt as if they were on fire. He tried to meet Elizabeth's eyes, but she wouldn't look at him. He saw Nicole's eyes appeal to him for help. But there was nothing he could do, and he carefully schooled his features to reveal nothing.

Danny's nostrils flared as he fought a moral battle with himself. He gave Tom a long, long look.

112

Tom met his gaze squarely. Everybody needed to do the right thing as they saw it. If telling Jason what he knew about Tom and Nicole was Danny's idea of the right thing to do—that was up to Danny.

"I thought they needed more time because it seemed to me that they were rushing into this thing, and . . ." He shrugged. "It just didn't seem like a really great idea," he finished lamely.

The two policemen frowned and Isabella covered her face with her hands, as if Danny's stupidity simply defied comprehension.

Elizabeth stared at her shoes.

Jason stared right at Danny. His open, friendly face didn't look open and friendly anymore. It looked angry and hostile. "Danny, I'm totally furious. You stepped over the line, pal. Way over the line. I'm not the little kid down the block anymore. I'm a grown man, and I make my own decisions. Got that? I didn't need to ask for my parents' permission to get married. And I don't need to ask for yours, either. Under the circumstances I think you'll understand that I'd rather have another best man."

He turned toward Tom and gripped his hand. "Tom. You're a new friend. But you're a really, really great guy. Will you do me the honor of acting as my best man at my wedding?"

Danny couldn't believe it. He just couldn't believe it. Of all the nutty, weird, unfair horrendous twists of fate—this was the nuttiest, the weirdest, and the most horrendously unfair.

He darted a look at Elizabeth to see how she was reacting. All the color was draining from her cheeks and her face looked dead white.

Nicole's hand flew to her throat and her mouth fell open in shock.

And Tom Watts—that *really, really great guy*—began to cough as if he had a chicken bone stuck in his clavicle.

Chapter
Ten

"There! Now are you happy? Now are you satisfied?" Isabella paced back and forth in Danny's cabin, madder than she had ever been in her whole life.

Danny sat on the edge of the bed and covered his face with his hands while she harangued him.

"Don't sit there looking put upon," she barked. "Look at the trouble you caused tonight. Police, no less." Isabella threw up her hands in frustration and shook her head. "See where interfering gets you?" she said, shaking a finger under his nose. "See?"

Danny lifted his head. "I wasn't interfering," he protested angrily. "I was intervening. There's a difference. Interfering is wrong. Intervening is a moral imperative."

Isabella angrily flipped her long hair off her shoulder. "Well, I can't see that the intervening worked out too well either. Jessica wound up sitting in some little island jail. Jason's furious with you and wants Tom to be his best man. Nicole is miserable over the whole situation. And so am I."

Danny groaned and hung his head. "Okay. Some of that is my fault," he admitted in a grudging tone.

"*Everything* is your fault," she practically roared. "Because you poked your nose into Jason's business."

Danny angrily stood. "Hey! Don't you think you're losing sight of the main issue here? *I* wasn't the one kissing somebody I wasn't supposed to kiss. If it was anybody's fault, it was . . ."

". . . yours," Isabella shouted, close to tears. "And the fallout from your mistake is affecting everybody else. Because you had to be Mr. Fix-It, Jessica wound up having to escape from some third-world lockup."

"Is she okay?" Danny asked, his handsome face suddenly worried.

"Who knows?" Isabella cried. "All we know is that she was last seen leaving the police station at a run."

The minute the police had tried to arrest Elizabeth for theft and illegal escape, Isabella had guessed what happened. Obviously the police had Jessica's description—which was exactly the same as Elizabeth's. So when they came onboard, they thought they had spotted their suspect.

116

But what made them think that Jessica took the ring in the first place? And how had she escaped from the jail? "And look what you put Elizabeth through," she said.

Danny groaned again. "Just thinking about Elizabeth makes me feel terrible," he said. "She's almost like a sister. I can't let Watts treat a sister of mine like that. And I can't let Jason marry a girl who's not in love with him."

"You don't know she's not in love with him."

"She was kissing Tom."

"So?"

"So people don't kiss people unless they're in love with them—at least not the way they were kissing." Danny covered his face with his hands. "I want to help everyone, but I just keep making a bigger and bigger mess."

Isabella walked over and stood in front of him. "Danny Wyatt, you listen to me. When we came on this cruise, you said what you really wanted to do was concentrate on me. And if you don't start minding your own business—our business—that means you and I are through."

"If minding my own business means closing my eyes while my best friends ruin their lives, then I'm sorry, but I can't do it," he said angrily. "And if having a sense of ethics means we're through—then I guess we'll just have to be through," he yelled, starting for the door.

"Where are you going?" she shouted.

"Someplace where I can think in peace," he shouted back, walking out of the cabin and slamming the door.

Isabella ran to the door and kicked it as hard as she could. Tears streamed down her face as a searing pain shot through her body.

Much later Danny crept along the hallway. He'd walked around the upper deck four times. Once his anger had worn off, embarrassment had set in. If he lived to be a hundred, he'd never stop being ashamed about what had happened in the ballroom. It was so humiliating that all he wanted to do was hide in the dark for a little while.

He had a flash of inspiration. He'd go to a movie. That way he could sit by himself in the dark and do some serious thinking.

Danny hurried to the entertainment deck. On the way he passed several SVU students, as well as some members of Jason's wedding party. Most of them smiled, but a few of them gave him strange looks.

He located the little movie theater and hurried toward the entrance.

"Good evening, sir," the usher said politely.

"How much is the movie?" Danny asked.

"No charge, sir. Once you're onboard, all entertainments are free of charge. Would you like to see *Rainy Weekend,* a French film about the tragic love affair between—"

Danny held up his hand, cutting him off. Tragic love wasn't something he was prepared to find entertaining at this point. "What's my second choice?"

"In Cinema II we have a fascinating documentary about the restructuring of the Venetian waterway system."

The film didn't sound action packed, but that was probably better. All he really wanted to do was think. Danny ducked inside a door with a neon sign reading CINEMA II over it. As his eyes adjusted to the dark he walked slowly down the aisle and slid into a row. There were very few people in the theater, but way down in the front he saw a couple making out.

He sighed, remembering how long it had been since he had Isabella in his arms. Why did things keep going wrong? Maybe Isabella was right. Maybe he should forget everything he had seen and heard. Instead of worrying about other people's girlfriends, he should focus on his own.

"Is anybody sitting there?" a familiar voice asked in a whisper.

Danny looked up and saw Nina standing beside him. "Danny! Is that you?"

"It's me," he whispered back. He pushed the seat down for her. "Here, sit down. Is the doctor coming? Want me to move over a seat?"

"No!" Nina said, her voice loud in the quiet theater. Then she gave Danny a guilty look. "No," she repeated in a hushed tone. "I'm, uh . . . sort of . . ."

"Hiding?" Danny asked in a low voice.

Nina nodded. "I am hiding. Rich is a great guy, but I needed a little time to myself."

"He does strike me as a guy who likes to talk."

"Mostly about himself," she said under her breath.

"Sounds like the guy's sort of an egomaniac," Danny whispered.

"Why shouldn't he have a big ego?" Nina demanded, obviously feeling defensive. "He's one of the youngest doctors in the country. He's a genius. He was through with high school by the time he was fourteen."

"Wow! So he must be a pretty interesting guy." Danny leaned closer to her so that he didn't have to raise his voice and disturb the other people in the theater.

"He is," Nina insisted. Then the corner of her mouth turned up a bit and she laughed. "He had to go back to the infirmary and check on a couple of things. Then we're supposed to take a moonlight walk. But in the meantime, I just needed a place to be where nobody could find me."

"Ditto," Danny said. "I just made a total fool of myself in front of every friend I ever had. Right now sitting in the dark is all I can cope with. Plus, I've been sort of ignoring Isabella, and now she's mad at me too."

Nina gave him a sour look. "Well, she should be. If Bryan could have just spent ten minutes thinking about me instead of . . . instead of . . ." She broke off and Danny saw her shoulders shake a little.

"Hey, Nina," he said softly. "Don't cry. We'll find Bryan, and—"

"It won't matter," she said quietly. "It's over between us."

"Well, at least you've got Rich," Danny said, trying to cheer her up.

Nina's shoulders shook even harder. "But he's not Bryan," she wept, taking the crumpled napkin that Danny offered her. "I would trade all the doctors in the world for one Bryan."

Danny sighed. "Bryan's a complicated guy." He was silent for a few moments. "I guess all people are complicated. And that's why relationships are complicated."

"I always thought your relationship with Isabella was simple," Nina said. "You two are crazy about each other—end of story."

"It is simple. At least, it used to be. But I'm going to have to do some serious damage control if I want to hear her say 'I love you' again."

"Do you think relationships are *supposed* to work?" Nina asked, her voice trembling.

"What do you mean?"

Nina lifted the napkin to her eyes and Danny put a comforting arm around her. "You can talk to me," he said. "You know anything you tell me in confidence goes with me to the grave."

Nina took a deep breath. "Well," she began in a small voice. "I've sort of developed this philosophy about life—the things that are right for you feel easy. If you don't feel the fit, maybe there's a reason."

"So?"

"So Bryan and I have to work so hard at getting along. It doesn't feel easy. It's not a good fit. Maybe I should quit crying over him and concentrate on Rich."

"Is Rich a good fit?"

"A perfect fit." She sighed unhappily. "That's the problem. There's no conflict—everything's fine between us. But that's all it is. *Fine*. It's not terrible. It's not wonderful. It's not . . ."

". . . not like falling forty floors into a pool of Jell-O with your arms around the person you love most in the world?"

Nina glanced at him. "Something like that."

"That's what being with Isabella is like for me," Danny said. "It's so incredible . . . the thought of us breaking up makes my blood run cold."

"So make up with her."

"It's not that easy," he said. "For me to make up with her, I'd have to compromise on something that's important to me. Something that's central to my whole system of ethics."

Nina groaned. "What is it with men? You sound just like Bryan. Everything's a control issue—you've got to prove you're right because of some *male dignity* thing."

"This has nothing to do with male dignity. It's got to do with human dignity and standing up for what's right."

Nina leaned her head back. "You're right. Relationships are complicated," she said.

He nodded.

"I'm glad I found you. I was feeling pretty lonely."

"Believe me, Nina, you're sitting next to the loneliest guy on the ship."

She looked at him and smiled. "The sweetest, too."

"And according to Isabella, the dumbest," Danny said unhappily.

Nina laughed, giving him a sisterly kiss on the cheek. Then they settled down to watch the rest of the movie.

Jessica watched Nina and Danny through eyes still heavy with sleep. The movie soundtrack had lulled her to sleep, but she had been awakened by the sound of a whispered conversation a few rows in front of her.

At first she had thought she was dreaming when she saw Danny and Nina sitting together. She had wanted to move closer so she could hear what they were saying, but then she realized that they would probably notice her if she stood.

At least she had a perfect view of them. They looked very romantic: Danny's arm was around Nina and her head lay against his shoulder. Just a couple of seconds ago, she had kissed him.

Jessica wondered if Isabella had any idea there was something going on between the two of them.

And I thought I was a big flirt, Jessica thought wryly. *Nina Harper makes me look like an amateur.* It seemed as though Nina was determined to cozy up to every eligible man on the ship.

Jessica looked at her watch. She'd been in the movie theater a long time. The dance had probably been over for hours, and she had no idea what had happened after she eluded her pursuers. It was time she snuck back to her cabin to see what was going on.

Very carefully, Jessica tiptoed out of the movie theater. There was no one in the lobby, and the decks and stairwells were quiet. She didn't pass anyone as she walked quickly to her cabin.

Jessica slipped in and saw Elizabeth staring gloomily out the porthole. When Elizabeth saw Jessica, she jumped to her feet and threw herself into her sister's arms. "*Where* have you been?" she demanded in a furious tone. "You can't believe what's been going on around here."

"Oh yes, I can," Jessica said, returning

Elizabeth's embrace. "This has been the most bizarre night of my life." She released Elizabeth and threw herself on her narrow bed. Then Jessica filled Elizabeth in on how her guardian angel had gotten her released from prison.

When Jessica had finished her story, she listened, fascinated, while Elizabeth related the tale of her own arrest and Isabella's eleventh-hour rescue.

"Danny had the ring all along," Elizabeth explained in conclusion. "He claimed it was stolen because he didn't think Jason would get married without it." Elizabeth paused, sighing. "Oh, Jess. It was just awful. He was forced to explain the whole thing in front of Jason and Nicole and a whole bunch of other people who were at the dance. He was totally humiliated."

"What did Jason do?"

"He got mad at Danny for interfering. Then he fired him as his best man."

"You're kidding."

Elizabeth shook her head. "And that's not all. Guess who he asked to take Danny's place?"

"Who?" Jessica asked, raising her eyebrows.

"Tom."

Jessica fell backward on the bed. "Unbelievable. What did Tom say?"

"I'm not sure. It was hard to tell through all that coughing."

"What about me?" Jessica asked. "Am I still on the Caribbean's ten-most-wanted list?"

"Nope. You're in the clear. But the police did ask if anyone knew of an individual who's passing himself off as a U.S. government official."

Jessica sat up eagerly. "Did anybody have information?"

"None," Elizabeth responded gloomily. She stood and reached for a cotton nightgown with red and blue flowers embroidered on the bodice. "I might as well go to sleep. This whole day has been a disaster. I'm just glad the cruise is almost over. At least a few of us are still speaking to each other."

"Exactly who *isn't* in a fight?" Jessica asked.

"Well, Danny and Isabella, I guess. They seem to be able to weather almost any kind of storm."

"I'm not so sure about that," Jessica said.

Elizabeth sighed. "I know they're bickering over Danny's position about Tom and me and this stupid ring business. Frankly, I wish Danny would make up with Tom. My problem with Tom's got nothing to do with him."

"Except that Tom was cheating on Danny's other best friend."

Elizabeth shook her head. "Then I wish Isabella would lay off Danny and not let this whole cruise go to waste."

"I don't think Danny is wasting it. And neither is Nina." Jessica lifted one eyebrow significantly.

Elizabeth gave Jessica a strange look. "What do

126

you mean by that?" Then she held up her hands. "Never mind. Don't tell me. I just can't worry about one more thing. I'm going to sleep. And if I had my way, I wouldn't wake up until it was time to go home!"

Jessica bit her lip and chewed thoughtfully as Elizabeth disappeared into the bathroom.

Chapter
Eleven

"You've got another split infinitive there," Bryan muttered as he proofread Jean's scholarship essay. He picked up the stub of a pencil that lay on the rough wooden table and began to erase, making dark smudges on the ruled paper.

"Where?" Jean asked. His brow wrinkled as he frowned at the paper, trying to read by the dim light of the lantern.

Bryan moved his finger down the heavily erasured essay and pointed at a sentence. "We talked about this before," Bryan reminded him. "Remember? In the paragraph about the impact of the new fishing methods on island economics."

Jean sat still for a moment, staring at the paper. Then his dark face broke into a smile. "Ah, yes. I remember now. How stupid of me to make the same mistake twice." He reached for the paper and picked up his pencil.

But Bryan put his hand down on the page. "Hey," he said in a kind voice. "Most of us have to make these kinds of mistakes over and over again before we learn the rules. Writing English is hard. It's a very irregular and idiomatic language."

"You are nice to teach me. And very patient."

Bryan laughed. "Patient—me? You're the one with the patience of a saint. How many times have I tangled the net in the boat? Five? Six? And you've spent hours teaching me to swim."

"It's very simple. I needed help on the boat." Jean chuckled. "I *had* to teach you to swim." Then his face grew more serious. "But swimming is easy. I just pushed you in and you taught *yourself*. Fishing is much harder. It takes a long time to learn to do it properly," Jean said. "You just need practice."

Bryan smiled and tapped the essay. "That's exactly what I've been telling you about writing this."

"We are teaching each other," Jean said happily, rolling up the threadbare sleeves of the old shirt he'd put on after the hard day of fishing.

Bryan turned his attention back to the essay. Jean had all the elements of a good writer. He was a critical thinker and had an analytical mind. And Jean had an emotional side to him that gave a dimension of humanity to everything he wrote.

"You're good," Bryan said, nodding to himself.

"I think we'll just correct this last sentence, copy it over, and call it a wrap."

"Hooray!" Jean said, grinning.

A sudden wind blew through the seaside cabin, extinguishing the candle on the table.

"I'll get a match," Bryan offered.

"No, wait," Jean said. "Sometimes it is nice to rest the eyes and enjoy the dark. Sometimes, too, it is easier to think without so many distractions." Jean was silent for a minute, staring out into the darkness. "You know, Bryan, that you are welcome to stay here as long as you like," he said finally. "But I suspect someone is waiting for you."

"I don't know about that," Bryan said sadly.

"If she is not, you must win her back."

Bryan was glad of the dark. It made it easier to admit to his own inadequacies. "How could I possibly get her back? The other guy is perfect. He's good looking. He's smart. And he likes to do all the stuff Nina likes to do. All kinds of water sports and stuff like that. On top of that, he's a *doctor*."

"Why does Nina need a doctor? Is she ill?"

Bryan laughed. "I guess we've got a culture gap thing here. In my country, a doctor is considered a very good catch."

"Same here," Jean assured him. "I was teasing you. Well, my friend, you are right. A handsome doctor who shares all of her interests is tough competition. So what are you going to do?"

"I can't complete medical school in time to go back to the ship."

"No."

"My looks aren't going to change too much."

"You could shave."

"Shave?"

"It's important to shave."

"Really?" Bryan lit the candle and then went over to the mirror and examined his two-day beard. "Wow. I am looking pretty scruffy. May I borrow your razor?"

"Of course."

"What else can I do?" Bryan asked.

Jean stared down at his paper and began erasing with an enigmatic smile. "I think you should sleep on it. The answer will come to you."

Bryan rolled his eyes. "Oh, great. This is all the advice I get—shave and get some sleep."

Jean laughed. "Never underestimate the power of sleep—or a clean shave."

Isabella pulled on her long, cotton jersey nightgown. She had to restrain herself from kicking the wall again. If she did, she'd hurt her toe again *and* she would bother the people in the cabin next door. "Oh, if only Denise were here. If only I had somebody sane to talk to."

Isabella went into the bathroom to wash her

face and brush her teeth. Maybe it was her mood, but she just couldn't shake the morbid fears that were beginning to crowd in on her.

There had been no word at all from Denise or Winston. According to Captain Avedon, it was a relatively simple thing to rendezvous with the ship at one of the other ports of call. All they had to do was follow the ship's itinerary.

So where were they?

Clearly the authorities in the area were concerned about pickpockets. Was it possible that Denise and Winston had been mistaken for pickpockets and were sitting in a jail somewhere— unable to contact either the ship or their parents?

Or worse, had there been some kind of accident? Were they lying in some tiny hospital?

Isabella stood and started for the door, determined to find the captain and insist that if Denise and Winston weren't found by tomorrow, he alert the international authorities and have them begin a search.

Then she remembered the look on the captain's face during the ring incident. He'd looked decidedly annoyed with everyone involved. Isabella had already inquired about Winston and Denise and been assured that they would be fine. He probably wouldn't appreciate her badgering him again.

Then she remembered the rather caustic remark he had made. *Your group doesn't seem to be having a very good time together. Perhaps they decided they would have more fun on their own.*

Maybe he was right.

"Fifty-three bottles of beer on the wall. Fifty-three bottles of beer. Take one down, pass it around, fifty-two bottles of beer on the . . ." Winston sang in a weak voice.

"Winston," Denise croaked.

"Mmmm?" Winston murmured, trailing his fingers over the side of the boat into the cool ocean water. If only it were clear water, and not salt water.

"Please stop singing about beer," she begged.

"Sure thing," he agreed in a flat, zombielike tone. Winston's croaking voice made a valiant attempt at a mellow tenor. "Moon River. Wider than a mile . . ." He broke off. "Sing along," he suggested.

"I'm not singing," Denise said irritably. "Not unless you can provide some water."

"I don't have any. But I thought maybe if I sang about liquids it would make us feel better."

Denise lay back miserably, resting her head on the side of the boat. "Life's funny. One minute you're in a boat, paddling toward an island. The next minute you're in the middle of the ocean with no land in sight, no paddle, no provisions, and a boat half full of water."

"It's my fault," Winston said gravely, laying his head beside hers. "I'm sorry I dropped the paddle. I'm sorry I don't have any water. And I'm sorry the boat is leaking."

Every muscle in his upper torso ached from bailing. They'd been scooping salt water out of the bottom of the boat for what seemed like hours. Finally, exhausted, they had decided to take a break and rest.

Denise smiled at his sad face. "It's both our faults. And I'm sorry I don't have any water either."

He lifted a weak hand and gestured upward. "Look at it this way. We may not have any water. We may not have any food. We may not have a paddle. But we've got this beautiful moon. And we've got each other." He turned over and pressed his body against Denise's. As he did, the boat lowered a bit and a small wave rolled in.

"Oh no!" Denise cried.

Both Winston and Denise sat up and began frantically to bail again.

"We're okay," Winston said, trying to keep the panic out of his voice. "We're okay. It's not that much water and we got it all out. We're okay. A-okay. Everybody got that? We're fine and dandy and . . ." His voice trailed off as he looked at something in the water. "We couldn't be better. We . . . uh . . ."

As Winston scanned the ocean, he felt Denise's

134

body tense. Her eyes were cutting left and right, as if she were watching a tennis match.

"We're going to be fine," he insisted. "We're alive. We're well . . ."

A third shadowy wedge joined the other two.

". . . surrounded by sharks, aren't we?"

"Uh-huh!" Denise answered.

"We're surrounded by one . . . two . . . three . . ."

Denise picked up the count. ". . . four . . . five . . . man-eating sharks."

"How do we know they're man-eating?" Winston asked. "Maybe they're not even sharks. Maybe they're friendly porpoises, and they're here to help us find our way home." He gave Denise an encouraging smile.

She smiled back. "Well, there's only one way to find out," she said wryly. "Personally, I'd be just as happy to let it remain one of those unsolved mysteries."

Winston felt the oddest sensation. It was in his face.

"Winnie!" Denise gasped. "What's wrong?"

Winston was experiencing the unthinkable. His permanent smile was fading away, and he felt as if it would never come back.

Denise took his hands. "What's the matter with your face? You look like you're having a stroke."

"Denise," he said softly, taking her hand. "Sit closer to me."

Denise carefully moved closer and Winston

stared dully at the fins that circled the boat. Then he turned his empty gaze toward her. "I'm all out of jokes. All out of songs." He kissed her cheek, relishing the softness of her skin. "If we don't make it out of this, I want you to know something."

Denise's eyes grew larger and her face looked unusually pale in the moonlight. "What?"

"You're the best thing that ever happened to me in my whole life." He paused. "What did I do to deserve you?" he whispered, almost to himself.

"You made me laugh," she said, lifting her hand and stroking his cheek.

She leaned forward and Winston wrapped his long arms around her. Denise sighed and held on tighter. "Winston. We can't give up," she insisted with a sob in her voice. "I'm not giving up, and neither are you."

Winston felt the muscles in his arms grow slack with fatigue. "I'm not giving up. I just need to rest."

Denise sighed heavily against his shoulder, and he felt her tired muscles tremble.

"You need to rest too."

She nodded.

"Let's lie down," he said softly. "We'll rest for a few minutes and then start bailing again. If we can keep it up until morning, maybe we've got a chance."

They'd had no fresh water in hours. They had

drifted so far off course, they were probably miles from any land. They were both at the end of their physical endurance. And they were surrounded by sharks. But Denise was right. They couldn't give up. "Lie down and go to sleep," Winston urged.

"We can't both go to sleep," Denise said.

"Okay, we'll sleep in shifts. You sleep first, and I'll wake you up in a little while."

Denise nodded and Winston pulled her down beside him, careful not to rock the boat. She lay with her head on his chest and her arms around him. "I love you, Winston," she said. "I love you more than I can ever, ever put into words."

"I love you too," he said, stroking her hair. "And I always will."

"What if I can't sleep?" she fretted.

"Shhh," he soothed. It had been a long, hot, emotionally grueling day. As soon as Denise relaxed, she would sleep.

Her hair felt like silk beneath his fingertips. And the smooth skin of her forehead felt like satin. Before long, he could tell from the gentle rise and fall of her shoulder that she was asleep.

Chapter Twelve

Who are you? Who are you? Who are you? The question repeated itself over and over in Jessica's mind, drumming through her brain in time with the rhythm of the engine.

She sat up, punched her pillow, and turned over with a flop. She shut her eyes tightly, determined to make another attempt at sleep.

But she was too keyed up. The events of the day kept flashing through her mind like a slide show. She examined every single image with her mental magnifying glass. Who was the tall dark man who had rescued her four times now?

Beneath her pillow, she could feel the vibration of the ship and hear the distant roar of the engine. *Who are you? Who are you? Who are you?*

It was getting hot in the small cabin. She turned again and kicked off the blanket.

Who are you? Who are you? Who are you?

She covered her ears with her hands.

Who are you? Who are you? Who are you?

It was no use. No matter what she did, the refrain kept repeating itself. To make matters worse, she could hear Elizabeth crying softly into her pillow.

Jessica punched at her pillow again. Should she say something to her twin? She could see Elizabeth on her bed; a beam of moonlight fell over her bunk and she lay perfectly still. It was obvious she was pretending to be asleep.

Even if Elizabeth had wanted to talk, Jessica couldn't think of anything very comforting to say. The cruise *was* turning out horribly. Winston and Denise had disappeared off the face of the earth. And Bryan had bailed out early on. Jessica had assumed it was because of the doctor. But maybe Bryan had known something that nobody else knew—that Nina had a crush on Danny.

Poor Isabella. Everybody thought she and Danny were such a perfect couple. Sure, they argued. But they argued the way parents did. It was the kind of bantering that took place between people who were secure in each other's love.

Jessica rolled onto her stomach, contemplating whether or not she should say anything to Isabella. The answer came quickly. *No.*

The whole reason Isabella and Danny were fighting was that Danny thought he should tell Jason about Tom and Nicole, and Isabella was insisting that the right thing to do was mind their own business. Isabella had made it crystal clear that she didn't like informers.

I won't say a word, Jessica resolved. *Even if it kills me.*

The minute she ceased her speculation about Isabella's love life, her own problems came rushing back.

Who are you? Who are you? Who are you?

Tears of frustration began to well in the corners of Jessica's eyes. But unlike Elizabeth, who liked to cry in private and pretend to be asleep, Jessica let out a loud, unhappy wail.

Elizabeth could ignore sighing and pillow punching, but she couldn't pretend she didn't hear Jessica wailing. Elizabeth sat straight up in bed. "Jessica!" she said, her voice concerned. "Are you all right?"

"No, I'm terrible!" Jessica said, her words muffled by her face in her pillow. "Somebody loves me. And I don't know who. He's a shadow. I can't dance with him or talk to him or kiss him or anything."

Elizabeth brushed away her own tears, got out of bed, and padded over to Jessica's bunk. "Maybe it's better. At least he won't cheat on you."

Jessica sat up and put her arms around Elizabeth. "I'm sorry things didn't work out with you and Tom. You were a great couple."

"I'm sorry too," Elizabeth answered tightly.

There was a knock on the door.

"I'll get it," Elizabeth said, releasing Jessica's shoulders and going to the door. When she opened it, she gasped. She'd never seen Isabella look anything but beautifully groomed and completely self-possessed—even when she was angry. But now her face looked paler than her white robe, and the dark circles under her eyes were almost black. She clutched a tissue in her hand, and her eyes were swollen and red. "I just can't be alone anymore," Isabella said. "That empty cabin is making me nuts. I keep imagining all kinds of awful things happening to Denise and Winston. And with nobody to talk to, I just get madder and madder at Danny for being so unreasonable."

"Come on in," Elizabeth invited. "We're up and sobbing too."

Isabella went over and sat on the foot of Jessica's bed. "Men are just impossible!" she said angrily. "You can't reason with them."

"You can't trust them," Elizabeth said.

"I can't even find one," Jessica said.

There was another knock at the door, and Alex entered before anyone had a chance to respond.

She wore a red flannel robe cinched around her small waist and her curly hair hung around her shoulders. Elizabeth had known Alex for years, but she had never seen her look so miserable and agitated. Her expression was distraught and her breathing was so shallow and rapid that Elizabeth was frightened. "What's the matter?" she cried.

"I just don't know what to do," Alex gasped. "I'm so uptight and . . . and . . ." Her breathing became even more rapid. "I'm having an anxiety attack," she wheezed, sitting down on the edge of Elizabeth's bed and putting her hand to her chest.

"She's hyperventilating," Jessica said.

"Should I get the doctor?" Isabella cried, jumping to her feet.

"No. Let's have her breathe into a paper bag," Elizabeth suggested. She went over to her suitcase and rummaged around for a bag of items she had purchased at the ship's gift shop. Elizabeth emptied the bag and handed it to Alex. "Just breathe in and out," she instructed. "Slowly."

"What happened to her?" Isabella asked softly.

"Her dream came true," Elizabeth said wryly. "And sometimes when dreams come true, they turn out to be nightmares."

"What does that mean?" Isabella asked.

Alex moaned unhappily. "I know what she means."

"Breathe," Elizabeth said, sitting down next to her. "Don't talk." She turned back to Isabella. "It means Alex always thought somebody like Leonardo was the man of her fantasies. And now here he is. And he's not the man of her fantasies after all."

Alex groaned again. "That's not quite it," she said between breaths.

"Breathe, don't talk," Elizabeth repeated. "I think she's upset because Leonardo wants to give her what she wants from Noah," Elizabeth explained.

"A modeling career?" Jessica asked.

Alex lowered the bag with a loud crackle. "No. Passion."

"Oh," Jessica said, crawling back into her own bed.

Elizabeth smiled at Alex, who was beginning to look a lot calmer. "Feeling better now?"

Alex shook her head. "No. I'm still completely confused. I feel like if I don't go with Leonardo to Italy, I'm giving up every romantic dream I ever had."

"Can't Noah make your romantic dreams come true?" Jessica asked softly.

"Apparently not," Alex said, her voice deepening with tears. "What does he care what I do? He probably wants me to go as far away as I can now that he's madly in love with Gin-Yung."

"Wow!" Jessica sighed. "No wonder you're bummed."

"Everybody's bummed," Isabella said darkly.

"Not quite everybody," Alex said in a disapproving tone.

The girls heard the high-pitched sound of a

giggle outside in the hallway. They hurried to the doorway, carefully peeking out.

Nina came strolling down the hall with her arm draped through Dr. Daniels'.

"Now there's a girl who knows how to make her own romantic dreams come true," Isabella said. "I know some people think she drove Bryan away by flirting with Dr. Daniels. But all I have to say about it is 'good for her'!"

Nina swallowed a yawn and wished she had taken a couple of aspirin before leaving her cabin to take a moonlight walk with Rich. Her head was pounding—mostly from listening to Rich talk and laugh.

His laugh! Ugghhh! It was like a foghorn.

Didn't he ever talk about anything but himself? His watch? His parents' expensive ski condo? His car? In his own words, he never settled for anything "less than the best."

It was true that he'd asked Nina a few questions about herself—but only enough to assure himself that she came from the "right" background.

It was becoming increasingly clear that he regarded her in the same light as his car and his watch. It was nice to know he considered her "top of the line," but on the other hand, it was insulting.

Where is Bryan? she wondered miserably.

She'd placed at least fifteen ship-to-shore calls for him, and she still hadn't been able to get in touch with him.

"And then, after we won the doubles at Wimbledon . . ." Rich was saying.

His voice droned on and on in the background as Nina's mind wandered freely. But she wasn't picturing Rich bounding over a grass court in white shorts; she was picturing Bryan bending over a makeshift card table in ragged jeans and no shirt—sweating in the heat while he struggled to get the BSU mailing out in time for the next election.

Commitment was sexy, Nina realized. And to some extent, so was distance. Her mother had always told her that guys didn't like girls who were too easy to get. The same seemed to be true for girls. She'd started taking Bryan for granted and lost interest in who he really was. She had started finding fault and wanting him to be something that he wasn't. She had forgotten that the things about him she thought she didn't like were the things that had attracted her to him in the first place.

Maybe it was true that familiarity bred contempt.

But it was also true that absence made the heart grow fonder. Now that Bryan was thousands of miles away and no longer hers for the asking, she wanted him more than ever. She appreciated him in a way she hadn't before. But deep down, she knew that no matter how much she missed him, she couldn't stay in a one-way relationship—a relationship where he wouldn't meet her halfway. If he loved her as much as she loved him, he would quit expecting her to make all the compromises.

"You and Nina both seem to have done pretty well in the love department," Jessica couldn't help commenting to Alex as the four girls sat cross-legged on the floor, sharing sodas, potato chips, and tissues. "I mean, no matter what you decide to do, it's pretty cool to have reeled in a handsome European who wants to make you a world-famous model." She laughed wryly. "I can't even get my mystery man to give me his name."

"I know," Alex said. "If this were happening to somebody else, I'd say what a great problem to have. But I feel like my heart is breaking. Literally." Her face contorted. "I've never been in so much pain in my life."

Elizabeth put a comforting hand on Alex's shoulder. "I wish I had some words of wisdom. But who wants wisdom from somebody stupid enough to be think her boyfriend was faithful?"

"You weren't stupid," Isabella protested.

"Yes, I was," Elizabeth said. "But if I hadn't seen it with my own eyes, I wouldn't have believed it."

There was an awkward pause, and Jessica stared at Isabella. She could hear Nina's laugh as she walked past their door with Dr. Daniels.

Jessica gritted her teeth. Nina was really something. It was pretty obvious that she had tried to use the doctor to make Bryan jealous. Now she was probably using the doctor to make Danny jealous.

And Isabella had no idea.

How could Isabella fight an enemy she didn't know she had?

I've got to tell her, Jessica decided. *But not here. Not in front of everybody. I'll tell her tomorrow—in private.*

Chapter Thirteen

Bryan and Jean Martin streaked across the glass surface of the ocean, leaving a white foamy trail. The Homecoming Queen shimmered in the distance.

As they got closer and closer, Bryan saw Nina standing on the uppermost deck with a pair of binoculars.

She was wearing a yellow sundress with a low neck and a full skirt. The sun gleamed on her smooth brown shoulders, and her braided hair was decorated with bright yellow and orange beads. Even from a distance of half a mile, Bryan could see her mouth pop open in surprise when she saw him in the speeding boat.

Nina fumbled with the binoculars, adjusting the focus. When he felt sure that she was focused squarely on him, he stood and pulled off the green polo shirt he wore over his white swimming trunks.

The boat came to a stop and Bryan waved at

Nina. Tentatively, hesitantly, she waved back.

He picked up the skis that were stowed in the boat and threw them out into the water. Then in a graceful movement he dove over the side.

"Bryan!" He heard her faint cry of alarm on the wind. But Bryan ignored it and easily fitted his feet into the water skis.

Jean threw him the rope and Bryan gripped the handle tightly. "Ready?" Jean called.

"Ready," Bryan answered.

The engine roared and the boat shot forward, pulling Bryan up out of the water, then setting him on his feet. He could feel Nina's shocked gaze as he skimmed over the water, light as a bird.

"You ain't seen nothin' yet," he yelled into the wind. He counted to three and then turned and skied backward, holding the rope behind the small of his back.

Seconds later in a deft motion he turned again, bringing his skis all the way out of the water.

Bryan glanced up at the Homecoming Queen. Quite a crowd had gathered to watch him. And standing in the middle of them, he saw a tall dark man in a bright white uniform.

This is for you, Dr. Daniels. Bryan lifted one foot out of the water, kicked off a ski, and slalomed up and down the length of the boat four times, taking the hairpin curves at top speed.

Even over the roar of the ship's engine he could hear wild applause and screams of approval.

Suddenly, from out of nowhere, a tall orange incline appeared.

Jean aimed the boat right at it.

"No!" he heard Nina scream. "Don't do it, Bryan. You'll kill yourself!"

Bryan smiled. A slow, grim smile.

He heard Nina's piercing shriek as he streaked out of the water and up the incline. For a moment he was airborne; then he smacked back down on the surface of the water.

The crowd went wild. Bryan skied up to the boat to take a bow and caught sight of Nina running down the outside deck stairs, her full yellow skirt floating in the wind.

The doctor ran behind her. "Nina," he called out in his deep voice. "Nina, come back. I'm a doctor."

"You're a quack," Bryan yelled.

The next thing he knew, Nina jumped into the water and her arms encircled him. . . .

"Wake up!" Bryan heard.

The powerful engine of the high-tech cigarette boat began to sputter out.

"Wake up," he heard the voice say again.

Reluctantly Bryan opened his eyes.

"Man," Jean said in a voice of disgust. "You were snoring so loud you sounded like a motorboat."

Bryan sighed heavily and turned over on his pallet. "Jean?"

"Mmmm?"

"Do you know anybody with a racing boat?"

Jean sat up on his bed and gave Bryan a funny look. "Oh, yeah. Sure, I know somebody with a racing boat. He tows it down to the water with his Rolls Royce." He snorted. "How would I know somebody with a racing boat?"

"Well, some kind of motorboat, then?"

Jean grinned. "I get you. You're still thinking about trying to impress your girl by waterskiing. But Bryan, it takes a long time to learn, and nobody has a fancy boat or—"

"Jean! I dreamed I was waterskiing. You said the answer would come to me in my sleep, and you were right. If I could ski up to the boat, Nina would see that . . . well . . . she'd see that I was at least *trying* to change for her."

Jean scratched his head and frowned. "Old Pierre has a motorboat and some skis. He used to take tourists out until they built the Calypso Spa. That's where the rich tourists go now. But the boat is very old." Jean laughed. "And so is Pierre."

"Think he would take me out tomorrow?"

Jean got out of bed, walked over to the shelf, and took down a coffee can. He pulled out a few bills and began to count.

Bryan jumped up, grabbing the money and stuffing it back in the can. "Forget that. I'm not taking any of your money."

"But we must pay him."

Bryan removed his watch. "Think he'll take this?"

Jean examined the watch and smiled. "For this, I think he'll give you the boat."

"This has been the longest night of my life." Tom sighed, settling down into the deck chair that had become his cot. Danny hadn't exactly locked him out of their cabin. But he was so hostile, Tom didn't want to sleep there.

It was warmer out here in the cold ocean air.

The dance had been over for hours, and Tom had gone back to his cabin only long enough to change into some loose, pajama-type pants and a T-shirt.

He lay on his back and looked up at the sky. Was there any such thing, really, as a wish upon a star?

If so, he'd wish that he had never, ever in a million years set foot on this ship. It was cursed. And this cruise felt as if it wasn't going to end. It was just going to get worse and worse—like some Wagnerian opera—until they were all dead.

He closed his eyes. On that positive note, he might as well try to sleep. Tomorrow would be a long day. It was going to be hard work acting as best man to a guy he'd stabbed in the back.

Tom sat up. "Good-bye, sleep," he said. Just thinking about Jason and Nicole and the wedding made his skin crawl. What a circus. Some people knowing what had happened. Other people not knowing. People would be whispering about him and Nicole. Elizabeth wouldn't speak to him. Jessica would glare at him. And so on.

The only person who would be glad to see him was the groom. It was so grotesquely ironic, Tom actually laughed out loud.

"What's so funny?" somebody asked in a flat voice.

Tom raised his eyes and saw Todd standing just a few feet away. He looked cold and antagonistic, his hands jammed down into his pockets and his jaw thrust out.

"Nothing," Tom answered curtly. "I don't owe you any explanations."

Todd took a step forward. "You hurt some-body I care a lot about," he said, removing his hands from his pockets. Tom noted that his fists were clenched.

Tom stood, recognizing the body language. "Not half as much as you hurt her, pal." Tom saw Todd's fist coming and ducked. Todd stumbled when he overshot the mark, and Tom punched him in the stomach.

Todd doubled over, breathing hard.

"Had enough?" Tom asked in a conversational tone.

Todd didn't answer; he came up out of the crouch and popped Tom in the jaw.

Tom reeled back, taken by surprise. "Hey! Watch it. This is turning serious."

Watching Todd move toward him again, Tom ducked in time to miss the next blow. Finally Todd turned and kicked a deck chair in frustration. "How can I hit you if you won't hold still?"

In spite of himself, Tom began to laugh. And so did Todd.

"Are we through fighting?" Tom asked. "Because if we are, I'm going to sit down. It's been a long day."

"We're through." Todd sighed. "Sit."

Tom sat down but Todd continued to stand, staring glumly off into space.

"I know that look," Tom said.

"What look?"

"The look on your face. The look that says 'I love Elizabeth Wakefield so much I want to die.'"

"I think you're describing your own face," Todd said, sitting down on the chair next to Tom's and placing his hands on his knees. "If that's the look you see on my face, it's just out of habit. I felt that way for so long, it's hard to stop."

"You don't love Elizabeth anymore?" Tom asked in surprise.

"I love Elizabeth, and I always will," Todd said quietly. "But I love her now more like a friend."

Tom's heart began to sink. "This is awful," he breathed. "Because she's in love with you, and . . ."

Todd shook his head. "No," he argued. "She's mad at you, so she turned to me. And I was stupid enough to be flattered and mess up something great."

"Gin-Yung?"

Todd nodded. "I'm crazy about her. But now she's hurt and angry. And it looks like she and Noah have got something going." He dropped his head into his hands. "Everything's a mess. I wish I'd never heard of the *Homecoming Queen*."

Tom began to laugh.

"What's so funny?" Todd asked.

"That's exactly what I was thinking when you walked up."

Todd lifted his head and stared at Tom. "What exactly is going on between you and Nicole?"

Tom opened his hands as if he were making a full disclosure. "Nothing. Absolutely nothing. We dated for a little while in high school. Jason was busy with Danny. They're old friends. They were happy to see each other. Elizabeth was looking after Jessica. Nicole and I started feeling like second-class citizens, and the rest is history. It was a kiss, Todd. That's it."

"And Jason doesn't know?"

"Not so far. But Danny's dying to tell him."

"So you want Elizabeth back?"

"Bingo."

"And I want you to have Elizabeth back," Todd said. "Not because I'm overly concerned about your happiness. But I'm concerned about *her* happiness. And for some strange, screwy reason she wants you."

Tom smiled broadly, as if he'd just heard great news. But he lifted his shoulders in a self-deprecating shrug. "There's just no accounting for taste, is there?"

Todd laughed reluctantly. Then he seemed to relax and laughed even louder.

"So what's your plan?" Tom asked with a smile. "How do I get her back?"

"Let's go to the all-night coffee bar," Todd suggested. "I'll buy you a cup of hot chocolate and tell you what I've got in mind."

Chapter
Fourteen

Uh-oh, Winston thought. *I fell asleep. I'll bet that means I'm dead. Good thing. Because if Denise realized I forgot to wake her up, she'd kill me.*

Winston could see the light through his closed eyelids. So far, so good. Everything he'd ever read about death said there was a bright light, and man, oh man, that light out there was bright. So he must be dead.

But weren't there supposed to be voices too? Voices summoning him into the light.

He waited, his eyes shut, wishing some booming voice would summon him. He was very impatient to open his eyes and take a look around. But he wasn't sure what the etiquette was in these matters. Death was a once-in-a-lifetime experience. He didn't want to do it wrong.

The light was strong. And hot. *Summon me, somebody. Please summon me. I'm cooking here.*

Cooking! Uh-oh! Maybe he wasn't where he'd hoped to be. Sure, he'd slipped up once or twice in life. He'd pilfered the odd pen. Told a white lie or two. He'd always considered those infractions pretty minor. Wow! The penalties for that stuff were a whole lot more severe than he'd anticipated.

Just as he was about to panic, Winston noticed the sound of waves and felt reassured. That was good. Water and waves were very eternal. Very spiritual. Not scary or punitive like the sizzling sound of bacon frying in a skillet.

He breathed a sigh of relief and relaxed. But then he heard something else. Sounds coming from above. Sounds that were far from celestial. Some kind of shrieking, screeching sound.

Still, he wasn't too troubled. The sounds weren't ominous. They were just noisy.

Winston felt a bead of sweat trickle down his face. Odd! He'd always assumed that . . . well . . . obviously it was time to stop assuming anything.

"Winston! Get up!"

Aha! Winston's eyes popped open and he saw Denise's face bending over his. "Denise!" he cried happily. "I'm so glad you're here. We're together, even in death."

Denise shook her head. "I don't think we're dead, Win. Get up and look. You're not going to believe this."

Winston sat up slowly and his jaw fell open. It was a few moments before he could speak. And when he found his voice, all he could do was gasp. "My gosh! It's . . ."

"It's paradise," Denise breathed in an awed voice. She was sitting up beside him in what was left of their leaky boat.

But it didn't matter that the boat was now a wreck. They weren't dead. And furthermore, they had washed ashore on the most beautiful island Winston had ever laid eyes on.

No photograph, movie, or descriptive passage in any book he had ever read even began to describe the vivid beauty that was spread out before them.

Winston stood, slowly and reverently. "It's like Eden."

"Completely unspoiled," Denise whispered. "And completely uninhabited. Listen. No cars. No horns. No radios. Nothing."

"How did we get here?" he mused, rubbing his forehead.

Denise turned and gazed at him with large and loving eyes. "I love you, Winston."

"I love you too."

"I think our love is so strong that the power of it brought us safely through the night," she said softly.

Winston swallowed, too moved to speak. It wasn't like Denise to philosophize. Usually he was the sentimental one, and she was the down-to-earth commonsense type.

Maybe, finally, they had found a setting in which Denise's romantic impulses would match his own.

"Come on," she said quietly, leading him into the dense foliage. "Let's find water and something to eat."

Feeling like Adam, Winston followed her and wondered if Eve had been half as beautiful as Denise looked now.

"Thanks for letting me share your cabin," Tom said, arranging his stuff around the litter of Winston's clothes and toiletries. "It was nice getting a few hours' sleep on a bed instead of a deck chair."

Todd smiled and buttoned his crisp white shirt. "Hope you're feeling good and rested. You've got a busy day ahead of you."

Tom rummaged through his suitcase until he found his own formal shirt, carefully folded in tissue paper. He grimaced as he unfolded the starchy cotton and began unbuttoning the little buttons. "This is my best shirt. I guess after this afternoon I can kiss it good-bye."

Todd laughed and grabbed the shirt out of Tom's hands. "If getting Elizabeth back isn't worth the price of a shirt to you, then you don't deserve her."

Tom laughed too and took the shirt from Todd. "I'm just looking for excuses to back out. What seemed like a good plan at two A.M. last night seems sort of like lunacy now."

Todd swung his tie over his neck and began looping it over. "Relax. It's a solid plan. Well thought out—by me." He tightened the knot in his tie. "I already saved your hide once, Watts."

Tom reached for his own tie. "Okay. You're a mastermind. I admit it."

"So let's go through it one more time," Todd said. "The wedding is over. People are standing out on deck at the reception. I take Elizabeth's arm. We walk up to say hello. I start a phony argument, give you a little shove, and . . ."

". . . I go overboard and Elizabeth jumps in to save me," Tom finished.

"Right," Todd confirmed.

"Because when she sees me flop around in the water and start going down for the third time, she'll realize how important to her I am."

"Theoretically," Todd said.

"Theoretically?"

"Well, there's always the outside chance that she'll cackle with glee and start applauding."

"Ha ha!" Tom felt a sinking feeling in the pit of his stomach. "Relax. If she doesn't jump in to save you, somebody else will."

"Are you volunteering?"

"No way. I've got my own problems to solve."

161

"Gin-Yung?"

Todd nodded. "Noah's a good guy. But if I can, I'm going to get him out of the picture. I want Gin-Yung back."

Tom looked at Todd's tie and frowned.

"What are you looking at?" Todd asked.

"Your tie."

"What's the matter with it?"

"It looks just like mine."

"So?"

"So we can't wear the same thing."

Todd rolled his eyes, picked Tom's blue blazer up off the bed, and threw it at him. "Come on. We've got a wedding to go to."

Isabella was pulling her black dress out of the closet when there was a knock on the door.

"Come in," she called.

The door opened and Jessica entered wearing a flowered, strapless silk sundress and a large straw hat. "Great outfit," Isabella said.

"Thanks." Jessica sat down on the bed. "What are you wearing?"

Isabella held up her long black dress. "Same thing I wore last night. With this . . ." She reached into the closet and pulled out a large black hat with a black rose on the brim.

"Black for a wedding?"

Isabella shrugged. "Sure. Why not? Anything goes these days, and to tell you the truth, black

162

suits my mood." She removed her silk robe and pulled the flowing dress on over her satin camisole. "I had big plans for this dress," she said in a sour tone. "Dancing with Danny in the moonlight. Strolling on deck. Feeling like Ginger Rogers."

She stuck the hat down on her head and turned to Jessica. "And on top of everything, I'm worried to death about Winston and Denise. I can't believe there's no message from them this morning."

Grumpily she turned to her dressing table and began poking around.

"What are you looking for? If it's your key, I think I'm sitting on it." Jessica moved over slightly and removed the sharp object that had been digging into the back of her thigh.

"Thanks," Isabella said, putting the key next to her purse. Jessica bit her lip hard as she watched Isabella apply the finishing touches to her makeup. She'd come to Isabella's cabin to tell her that she had seen Danny and Nina looking very cozy together in the movie theater.

But Isabella's mood was already so bad, Jessica couldn't bring herself to make it worse.

She watched Isabella moodily pin her hair up under the hat in a forties-style roll. It was very glamorous. "Maybe it's my fault. Maybe I'm losing my touch," Isabella mumbled through a mouthful of hairpins. "Maybe I'm just not desirable anymore."

"You are too," Jessica protested immediately.

Isabella leaned closer to the mirror, removed a pin from her mouth, and stuck it savagely into her hair. "I'm ugly."

"Isabella!"

"I'm mean and short-tempered . . ." A tendril of hair slipped out of the pin. She threw it against the wall and burst into tears. Jessica jumped up and put her arms around her. "Isabella, stop it. You know you're beautiful and sophisticated and everybody thinks you're wonderful."

"Then why is everything so awful between me and Danny?" Isabella choked.

Jessica patted her friend's shoulder. She hated to see Isabella so upset, but when push came to shove, it was difficult to tell her that the problem wasn't with her. The problem was that Danny was involved with somebody else.

Danny gritted his teeth in irritation as jovial male voices passed down the hall outside his cabin. That was about the fourth group of people who had gone down the hall singing that same stupid "Get Me to the Church on Time" song from *My Fair Lady*.

He stood in front of the closet, thinking. Should he even go to the wedding? If he did, he wouldn't have any fun. But if he didn't, he might just look childish.

He pictured Isabella's angry face. If he asked

her, she'd tell him to go to the wedding and be a good sport.

He didn't feel like being a good sport, but he was tired of feuding with Isabella. He reached for his blazer and tie. Maybe they could make up at the reception and finally do some of the dancing she'd been looking forward to.

Alex buttoned the row of tiny jet buttons that closed the bodice of her lavender print Victorian dress. Her hair was freshly washed, and she had combed it carefully so that the auburn curls framed her face and flowed over her shoulders.

It was a perfect wedding outfit. She had never looked better. She had never looked more romantic. And she had never felt more miserable.

The door opened and Leonardo swept in. Alex noticed that he didn't bother to knock. He had a fiercely possessive nature and seemed to take it for granted that he would be welcome in her cabin.

Alex knew she should be annoyed. But she wasn't. It was exciting to feel so important. She just wished it was Noah who was sweeping into her room with a wicked and possessive gleam in his eye.

Leonardo wore a white silk shirt. She could see the outline of his dark beard even though he had shaved only hours before. He put his arms around Alex's waist, bent her backward, and kissed her hungrily.

Alex's arms reached up and wrapped around his neck. She pressed her lips against his. His breathing quickened and his lips moved passionately over her mouth.

If somebody took our picture, Alex thought, *we'd look like the models on the cover of a romance novel.* But it wasn't real. At least not for her. She felt a sense of ego gratification—but it wasn't the heart-stopping, palpitating breathless passion she craved. She wanted glamour. She wanted romance. She wanted passion. But she wanted it with Noah.

Leonardo lifted her to her feet and released her. He took a step back and gazed at her with admiration. "You look beautiful."

"Thank you," she said softly, turning slightly away in embarrassment. His admiration made her feel self-conscious. Was this what it felt like to be a model?

He reached into his pocket. "I brought you something."

She turned toward him, curious to see what was in the small soft cloth he was unfolding. He turned back the last corner of the bottle green velvet and she gasped. "Leonardo! No!"

It was a pair of earrings. Two smoky diamonds suspended from a fine mesh gold setting.

"Yes," he said. "They are for you."

"I can't accept them," she whispered, taking a step back.

He made a gesture of impatience. "These.

They are nothing. I bought them on the island. For now they will do—later you will have nicer things. I will see to it. But I think these are pretty, and they suit your coloring."

With a shaking hand, Alex reached out and took one of the earrings from him. She went to the mirror and held it up next to her ear. It was, indeed, beautiful. And the color was perfect.

Leonardo appeared behind her, staring at her reflection over her shoulder. He lowered his head so that his face was even with hers. "Yes. I knew they would be perfect. Come, quickly, put them on," he said imperiously.

Alex hurried to put the earrings on, wishing she could take more pleasure in them.

Outside, they heard a group of laughing students go by.

"It is getting late," he said. "We should be going."

She took a last look at her reflection, and they hurried out of the cabin. Just as Leonardo was pulling the door closed Noah came out of Gin-Yung's cabin, with Gin-Yung behind him. Noah stared at her and Gin-Yung smiled widely as the two couples met.

"Hello," Leonardo said cordially.

"Hi," Noah answered.

Alex eyed Gin-Yung's outfit. Khaki skirt. White shirt. Blue blazer and loafers. Her heart sank. If this was what Noah wanted in a woman, it just wasn't Alex. And it never would be.

"Wow!" Gin-Yung commented. "Are those the earrings I saw in the window of Mia's Jewelry?"

Leonardo nodded and Alex swallowed hard. Mia's Jewelry! She'd had no idea. That was one of the most expensive jewelry shops in the Caribbean. She hadn't dreamed that . . .

Noah's face looked pained, and he and Gin-Yung exchanged a look. Alex suddenly felt overdone and embarrassed. Her outfit was excessive and so were the earrings. "See you later," she said quickly.

Alex took Leonardo's arm and began hurrying up the hallway. Okay. This was it. She was through pining over Noah. Clearly she wasn't Noah's type. As much as she cared about him, she wasn't going to let any man turn her back into plain old Enid Rollins.

Leonardo saw her the way she wanted to be seen. And he adored her. She would go to Italy. She would have the exciting, wonderful life she had always wanted. And she would be beautiful, and wear beautiful clothes, and surround herself with beautiful things.

Eventually she would return Leonardo's passion. It was only a matter of time.

"Alessandra, darling," she heard Leonardo say. "Why are you crying?"

She lifted her hand and fiercely wiped a tear from her cheek. "Weddings always make me cry," she explained.

* * *

"I think we should give up," Gin-Yung said glumly as they entered the ballroom. "We haven't got a chance."

Waiters circulated with glasses of punch on silver trays. Noah took two and handed one to Gin-Yung. "Don't do this to me," he begged. "We're supposed to be a mutual-support system. You're not holding up your end."

Gin-Yung tapped her loafer on the floor and took a sip of her punch. "I'm just trying to face facts. We're outclassed." She nodded toward Elizabeth, who stood next to Todd—tall, elegant, and exquisite in a raw-silk blue dress. Her long tan legs looked even longer than they had last night. Her blond hair was caught back loosely in a blue bow.

"Look at her." Gin-Yung looked down at her own outfit. "And look at me. If you were Todd, who would you choose?"

Noah gave her a kind smile. "I'm not Todd, so I can't answer that."

"No," she said bluntly. "And you're no Leonardo, either. Do you have any idea what those two perfectly matched diamonds must have cost?"

Noah shook his head. It was all he could do not to groan and sink to his knees in depression. "Okay. You're right. We're totally outclassed. Or at least I am. You can always buy a pouf dress. But

I can't give a girl perfectly matched diamonds."

"I looked stupid in that pouf dress," she said morosely.

"No, you didn't. You looked very pretty."

"Well, it's academic," she snapped. "Because I was so mad when I got back to my cabin after the dance, I stomped all over it. The dress didn't get Todd's attention at all. He spent the whole night protecting Elizabeth from the police and didn't even seem to notice me." She gloomily ground her toe into the floor.

Noah reached into his pocket, felt around in its depths, and removed something. "I'm no expert like Leonardo. But I think you look very pretty with or without a poufy dress. And I think you deserve something nice. Here. These aren't diamonds, but they *are* perfectly matched and they just might bring you luck."

"What are they?" she asked.

He opened his hand to reveal two pennies. "One for each loafer," he explained solemnly.

Chapter
Fifteen

Lila smoothed the folds of her peach silk dress. The top was frothy and sheer, with a peach-colored camisole beneath it. The skirt was made of layered peach silk gauze.

Her broad-brimmed hat was trimmed with a large peach flower. On her feet she wore high-heeled sandals.

It was a perfect dress to wear to a wedding. For that matter it would be a perfect dress to get married in. In fact, it wasn't very different from the dress she had worn when she married Tisiano.

She'd worn a veil instead of a hat. And silk pumps instead of sandals. But her wedding dress had been diaphanous and contemporary; Tisiano had said she looked like a nymph.

It hadn't been purely accidental that she had brought this dress to wear to the wedding. Dresses like this made her feel romantic and young and . . .

171

She reached up and removed her hat. It felt completely unsuitable now. It was too frivolous for a widow. Lila hurried to the closet door and flung it open.

Minutes later she had changed into a somber navy-blue linen dress with navy pumps and a heavy gold chain around her neck.

She looked like somebody's mother, but so what? At least she looked dignified. Leonardo couldn't accuse her of dishonoring Tisiano now.

Lila stuffed Kleenex, keys, and lipstick into a navy-blue clutch bag and left her cabin, hurrying down the hall.

She felt a slight worried thump in her chest. This would be the first wedding she had attended since her own. Would she be able to bear it? Or would it bring back painful memories?

As she neared the ballroom Lila could hear baroque music playing. The strings and trumpet brought the memories back in a flood. The images were so sharp and vivid that they almost took her breath away. It was the same music that had welcomed the guests to her own wedding. She swayed on her conservative one-and-a-half-inch heels.

"Lila! Are you all right?" Bruce was suddenly beside her and his arm encircled her waist.

"I'm all right," she said softly, realizing as she said it that she was far from all right. She fell into his shoulder, feeling dizzy.

"Come over here and sit down," he urged.

Bruce guided her toward some chairs that sat against the rail, where cool air came up off the ocean. "Sit down. You'll feel better in a minute."

Lila took some deep breaths. The sharp, salty air was bracing, and within moments she felt better.

"Is there a problem?" Bruce asked softly. "Do you want me to get anybody for you?" He took her hand and felt her pulse.

Lila had tried hard to avoid Bruce's gaze. But now she turned her face toward his and their eyes met. His face moved nearer to hers, his eyes pleading. "Lila," he began. "This is ridiculous. We need to be together. We belong together."

Her heart began to melt and her legs felt wobbly. Bruce was the sexiest guy she had ever known, and her arms ached to hold him. But Lila pulled her hand from Bruce's and stood abruptly. Across the deck Leonardo stood with Alex and a group of guests—glaring at her.

"Thank you. I'm fine now," she said quickly, hurrying away from Bruce as fast as her legs would carry her.

Bryan let go of the rope as they neared the dock. He sank gently into the water. The ancient motorboat came to a sputtering stop at the edge of the dilapidated dock, where Jean stood applauding. "All right! Bryan. You did it! You water-skied."

They'd been out for three hours and Bryan couldn't believe how easy waterskiing had turned out to be. He was no expert. And he was years away from slaloming up an incline the way he had in his dream. But he didn't see any reason why he couldn't catch up with the *Homecoming Queen* and ski a big circle around it.

Old Pierre turned in the boat, his eyes twinkling in his weather-beaten face. "Bryan. You learn real quick. Someday, with practice, I think you will be very good."

"Someday is today," Bryan said, swimming toward the ladder and climbing out of the water.

"Eh?" old Pierre asked.

"He needs to rendezvous with the *Homecoming Queen*," Jean explained.

"The cruise ship?"

Jean and Bryan nodded. "We brought his suitcase," Jean said. "We were hoping you would take him out. He wants to ski up to the boat."

Old Pierre shook his head. "This boat is old. The ship is many miles away. I don't know . . ." he said uncertainly.

"Pierre," Jean wheedled. "You have to take him."

"I'm old and very tired," he answered.

"Please," Bryan begged.

"It will take a lot of gas. It is too expensive."

"Expensive!" Jean cried. "The man has given you a very good watch. You can sell it and buy fifty tanks of gas."

Old Pierre turned to Bryan. "Why do you want to leave here? You're having a good time." He gestured to Jean Martin. "You have a good friend. What's on the boat that we don't have here?"

"A girl," Jean said finally. "He wants to ski up to the boat and impress a girl."

A slow grin spread across old Pierre's face. "Well, then. Why didn't you say so? Of course we must go."

Bryan let out a shout of joy, and Jean grinned broadly as he swung Bryan's suitcase into the old motorboat. "Well," he said to Bryan. "I guess this is it."

Bryan felt a catch in his throat. "How can I ever thank you?"

"You have thanked me. By helping me with my essay."

Bryan felt overwhelmed. He'd never met anyone so generous and kind. As they hugged good-bye, Bryan realized he had learned far more from Jean Martin than just how to swim and to ski.

He'd learned that other people's feelings were more important than his own dignity. He'd learned to take a risk. He'd learned how to be more of a man. "See you next fall," Bryan said thickly, wiping a tear from his eye.

"Next fall?" Jean repeated in a curious voice. "Will you be coming back next fall?"

Bryan shook his head. "No. I expect to see you at the University of Miami. You'll be a freshman there—and the BSU convention is being held on that campus next October. Maybe you'll put me up again?"

Jean smiled and held up his crossed fingers. "If I get accepted, you can count on it. And I won't make you fish for your keep," he added with a laugh. The boys shook hands warmly, then slapped each other on the back.

"Hurry, hurry," old Pierre urged, tinkering with the ancient motor. "We've got a long way to go."

Bryan climbed carefully down into the boat as Pierre turned on the engine. The old boat let out a tremendous roar and sped away. Behind him, Bryan saw Jean lift his hand and wave. Bryan waved back until Jean was nothing but a speck on the horizon.

Denise fell on her stomach and drank thirstily from the clear, babbling brook. Never had water tasted so delicious. Beside her she could hear Winston quenching his own thirst.

He took a last gulp, then thrust his whole sunburned face and head into the cool water. He pulled out his head and threw it back with a joyous whoop, letting his wet mane send an arc of water shooting high into the air.

Denise lifted her face from the pool, then turned over and lay on her back. "It's unbelievable. Fresh water. Shade."

He leaned over and kissed her softly. "And we're together."

She smiled. "And we're together," she repeated. She gazed at her surroundings with awed eyes. Everywhere she looked were exotic blooms, vivid colors, lush plant life.

The smells from the flowers were so heady that she felt intoxicated. Not only by the beauty surrounding them, but by the presence of Winston.

She'd never seen a man look sexier, more natural, or more desirable—even with a sun blister on his nose.

He kissed her softly again, his lips warm and eager. Soon they were rolling over and over in the thick undergrowth.

"Denise," he whispered in a husky tone.

"Yes?" she whispered back.

"Are you thinking what I'm thinking?"

"It depends," she said breathily. "What are you thinking about?"

A deep rumbling sound from his stomach broke the heavy, tropical silence. "I guess I'm thinking about food," he admitted.

Denise sighed and sat up. The thought she had been pushing to the back of her mind shoved its way to the front. "Me too. In fact, I'm starving."

He stood, took her hand, and pulled her to her feet. "Let's see what we can find to eat in paradise."

"I don't think we're going to need to look far." She pointed. "Look. Mangoes. Growing right on a tree."

Winston whistled. "I can't believe it. It's amazing. Food for the taking." Moments later he was shinnying up the mango tree. He plucked the ripe fruit and used his shirt as a sack to collect them.

"Careful!" Denise cautioned.

He dropped to the ground, shirtless, barefoot, and sunburned.

Feeling like a Polynesian princess, Denise took the mango he offered, savoring the juicy lush fruit. For the next several minutes they feasted in silence.

When they were finished, Winston took her sticky hand in his and gazed deeply into her eyes. "Denise," he whispered. "If we have to stay here the rest of our lives, that's fine with me. This is as close to paradise as I'll ever get in this world. And I can't believe you're here with me."

"Oh, Winston," Denise murmured.

He leaned forward and Denise stood on her tiptoes to receive his kiss. His gold-tipped eyelashes fluttered downward. Just as their lips were about to meet, something whizzed by Denise's ear.

There was a cracking sound, and her eyes flew open in time to see Winston fall backward like a sack of potatoes. "Winston!" she cried. She was just lurching forward to help him when she heard someone shout *"Fore."*

Another whistling missile came whizzing through the brush. Denise felt something smack the back of her head. And then everything went black.

Chapter Sixteen

"What are those whistles?" Elizabeth asked.

"I think they're the nautical equivalent of wedding bells," Todd answered. "It means we need to find a seat. Sounds like it's show time."

He took her arm and they entered the ballroom, where folding chairs had been set up for all the guests.

Elizabeth Wakefield was one of the most beautiful girls in the world. But he was over her.

And he knew she was over him.

And she knew he knew she knew he was over her.

The sooner they ended this charade, the sooner they could both get on with their true romances. Hers with Tom. His with Gin-Yung.

Elizabeth sat up straight and did her best to look eager and happy. Even though she had sobbed half the night, a little creative concealer application had hidden the dark circles under her eyes. And by the time Todd had knocked on her cabin door, she had decided that she'd be able to at least *act* happy.

There was a flurry of movement as people hurried to take their seats. Elizabeth caught sight of Tom peering out the doorway at the front-left corner of the ballroom. As best man, it was probably part of his job to keep an eye on the guests. He'd let the wedding party know when everyone was settled and ready for the ceremony to start.

As soon as Tom's eyes fell on her, she forced her lips into a broad, flirtatious smile. "Oh, Todd. Don't you just love weddings?" She took his arm and leaned against him, looking up and fluttering her eyelashes.

She couldn't help cutting her eyes back in Tom's direction. His eyes met hers briefly, then he closed the door.

Lila sat clutching a Kleenex in her hand. *Leonardo was right about me,* she thought miserably. *I have no character. No emotional depth. I'm shallow and superficial and selfish and . . .* She lifted the tissue to her face and dabbed at her eyes.

It was improper to be so deeply in love with someone else so soon after Tisiano's death. It was in bad taste. It was heartless.

She bent her head miserably, almost wishing it

181

really had been she who had died and not Tisiano. Without him, and without Bruce, her life was unbearably lonely. And dull.

She would be good company for Tisiano's mother and his two maiden aunts, Leonardo had said. They lived quietly in the country and had very little company. They would enjoy having a young person there. Particularly one as attractive and vivacious as Lila.

Lila felt a tear trickle down her cheek. She didn't want to be company for Tisiano's mother and two maiden aunts. She didn't want to live quietly in the country. She didn't want to grow old in a foreign country with no one to love and no one to love her.

And the thought of sitting around moldering while Enid Rollins became an international supermodel, going to exciting parties and exotic places, was almost more than she could bear.

I won't do it, she thought rebelliously. *I won't. Leonardo has no power over me. He can't make me do something I don't want to do.*

She looked down and sneered at her own attire. *And furthermore, I'm not going to spend one more minute in this navy-blue dress.* She'd go back to her cabin and change. Lila stood up. Just then, the ship gave a tremendous lurch and a furious gust of wind blew through the ballroom.

The lights flickered, and Lila turned her head in time to see Leonardo bend over and kiss Alex's cheek. In the flickering light, his face looked exactly like Tisiano's.

"Relax, folks, relax," Captain Avedon's voice said cheerfully over the PA system. "We're just going over a little choppy water. There's absolutely nothing to worry about."

Lila's hands began to shake and she sat back down in her seat.

It was a sign. A sign from Tisiano. Leonardo might not have any power over Lila. But Tisiano still did.

"So after prep school, I debated with myself for about six months," Rich said as he and Nina took their seats. "Law or medicine? Medicine or law? I mean, I knew it had to be one or the other. Now, law was definitely the more lucrative route—assuming I went into plaintiff work. But my science grades were always excellent and I enjoyed biology and . . ."

Nina smothered another yawn. Rich had told her all this before. In fact, he'd told her three or four times. He'd told her *everything* three or four times.

It wouldn't have been so bad if all his stories didn't revolve around him and how great he was.

Oh, Bryan, Nina thought miserably. *Where are you and why aren't you here? And why, why, why did I ever think parasailing was more important than spending time with you?*

*　　*　　*

Danny folded his arms across his chest and stared stonily ahead. He had chosen a seat in the very back row. The wedding was anything but what he had envisioned when he'd first heard he was going on the cruise.

When Elizabeth had announced that they were all going on the luxury cruise, Danny had pictured nonstop fun, sun, romance, and fine dining. He'd been thrilled at the prospect of his old friends meeting his new friends. He'd expected the cruise to be a vacation he'd remember for the rest of his life.

He'd remember this for the rest of his life, all right. It would be pretty hard to forget the biggest disaster at sea since the sinking of the *Titanic*.

Isabella hurried in and took a chair several rows ahead of him. As soon as she was seated, she turned in her seat to survey the room. When her eyes met his, she lifted her chin a bit and turned back to face the front.

Danny sighed. What a total and complete fiasco. His girlfriend wasn't speaking to him. Jason wasn't speaking to him.

And *he* wasn't speaking to Tom.

A total and complete wipeout. Having a sense of ethics was a curse, he decided. He'd really been trying to do the right thing. And the result was that he had made everybody mad.

He'd never been so depressed in his life. He'd never been so angry, either.

The side door opened and Tom peered out again. Danny noticed that he had a white flower in the buttonhole of his jacket.

If anybody was going to be standing there as best man—which they shouldn't be, because Nicole was obviously too young and fickle to get married—it should have been Danny.

But even if Jason came striding out and *begged* him to be his best man, Danny would say no. In good conscience he couldn't stand up and support his old friend while he made the biggest mistake of his life.

Because Danny knew, deep down, that Jason and Nicole should not be getting married today. They were making a big mistake. Not only was Nicole too young; Jason was too.

At first Danny had been relieved that Jason hadn't changed a bit. He was still the same fun-loving guy he'd always been. But now Danny realized that Jason needed to do a lot of changing before he got married. He had a lot more growing up to do. They all did.

Danny jiggled his foot irritably and sighed. Well, he'd done everything he could to try to stop it. To try to save them from a terrible mistake.

And had anybody thanked him?

No.

Jason had "fired" him. And Isabella had yelled at him.

Weddings were supposed to be fun. Danny felt more like he was at a funeral.

Jessica sat directly behind Leonardo and Alex.

She watched as Leonardo took Alex's hand and held it possessively. He whispered something in Alex's ear and Jessica watched her blush and then giggle.

Jessica slumped down in her seat and looked right and left. She was sitting between two girls she had never met before. They kept leaning over Jessica to talk to each other.

Jessica looked around, trying to spot a head and shoulders above the crowd that might belong to her guardian angel. But no one she saw seemed to fit the description.

"So then Glenda went to George's room and . . ." The girl on Jessica's right was speaking so intensely that she was practically leaning on Jessica's lap.

"Excuse me," Jessica said.

The two girls fell silent and gave her an inquiring look.

"Would you two like to trade places?" Jessica asked with a slight edge to her voice.

"No, thank you," the girl on the left said, taking the arm of the boy beside her. "I want to sit by my boyfriend. But thanks anyway."

"Me too," the girl on the right said. Jessica watched her take the hand of the male beside her in her hand and lace her fingers through his.

The sight of those clasped hands made Jessica's heart ache. She desperately wanted to hold someone's hand tightly. To lace her fingers through someone else's and exchange a knowing and intimate smile.

The two girls leaned back over Jessica to resume their conversation. Luckily they broke off as the wedding music started. The whispering group of guests immediately became quiet as Captain Avedon stepped from the side door and walked to the center of the bridal bower at a stately pace.

Jason and Tom followed behind him.

The music swelled and Jessica turned, along with everyone else, to watch the procession of ten bridesmaids walk up the center aisle.

Jessica instantly loved the bridesmaid dresses, which had a tropical theme. The girls wore brightly colored green, aqua, and pink silk sarong skirts that reached their ankles. Their silk tops were cropped and showed each girl's tanned midriff. Matching colorful scarves were tied island style around their heads.

Tendrils of blond hair escaped the scarf and framed the maid of honor's beautiful face. Trails of orchids spilled from her bouquet.

The second bridesmaid was dark. And the vivid colors of her dress and scarf made her look like a glamorous movie star.

Nicole obviously had a theatrical flair and a

sense of humor. Jessica found herself thoroughly enjoying the spectacle.

If I ever get married again, Jessica thought, *I'm going to have a wedding just like this. No tacky satin formals with portrait necklines. I want something individual and unique. Something people will remember.*

Jessica closed her eyes and pictured her own theme wedding. After Elizabeth, Lila, Isabella, and Denise had gone up the aisle, she would make her entrance.

She'd wear something green and filmy. She would look like a mermaid. And she'd have a hair ornament made from beautiful shells. She'd shimmer up the aisle, taking small steps with her fishtail skirt trailing behind her. Finally she would take her place next to someone tall and handsome with broad, broad shoulders.

After the vows were exchanged, he'd turn toward her to kiss her and . . .

Jessica ground her teeth in frustration. No matter how hard she tried to visualize his face, it was a blank. A total mystery. She knew his back. She knew his profile. But she had never seen him face to face.

Who are you?

Chapter Seventeen

"What's wrong?"

"Nothing is wrong," old Pierre assured him.

The engine coughed and sputtered again.

"It sounds like something's wrong," Bryan insisted. He glanced around. There was a lot of ocean and no land anywhere to be seen.

And the motorboat was no cruise ship. "Are you certain you know how to find the *Homecoming Queen?*" he asked in a worried tone. Old Pierre gave him a bland smile and a shrug. "Nothing in life is certain, young man."

As if to prove Pierre's point, the boat gave a groaning sputter and the motor abruptly fell silent. They came to a stop and drifted on the gentle current.

Unperturbed, old Pierre reached under the seat and removed a toolbox. Without haste he opened the lid and studied the contents, deliberating over the selection as if they had all day.

"It's really important that we find the ship," Bryan said in what he hoped was a galvanizing tone.

Old Pierre merely nodded.

"Because if I don't find it, I might just lose the greatest woman in the whole world."

The old man nodded again.

"And if I lose Nina, my life just won't be worth living."

Pierre removed a screwdriver.

"I mean, I just can't imagine going on without her. All the things I thought were so important don't seem as important now. Well, they *are* important. But you have to keep things in perspective, you know?" Bryan knew he was babbling, but he couldn't help it.

It was funny. He'd enjoyed the slow, calm island philosophy while staying with Jean. But the closer he got to his old life, the more wired he felt.

Suddenly something appeared on the horizon. Something large and white. The *Homecoming Queen*!

Bryan turned back to old Pierre. At this rate the ship would sail on by and disappear over the next latitude. It was time for a little uptight-urban-type-A-anal-retentive efficiency. "Here," he said briskly, dropping his recently acquired laid-back island demeanor. "Give me that." He snatched the screwdriver from old Pierre and tackled the motor as if his life depended on it.

*　　*　　*

Alex couldn't help being flattered. Ten absolutely gorgeous, sexy women had just walked slowly past them. And Leonardo had barely given them a glance; instead, he gazed at her.

Suddenly she sensed another pair of eyes on her. Alex turned and caught her breath. Noah wasn't staring at the lovely and shapely figures that were gliding up the aisle either. He was looking at her.

His usual calm look was gone and his eyes burned brightly. Maybe she was wrong about Noah. Maybe he did still care about her.

But as she watched, Gin-Yung touched his arm. Noah bent his head to catch her words, and they laughed softly.

Alex's heart began to ache. They looked so in tune. So down to earth. So practical.

Why couldn't Noah just do one crazy, volatile, impractical, passionate thing?

Just once.

The music swelled and the back doors to the ballroom were flung open with a dramatic flourish by two liveried stewards in white.

Danny drew in his breath when he saw Nicole standing just inside the ballroom, surrounded by a sea of shimmering white satin with tiny seed pearls sewn over every square inch. She looked breathtakingly beautiful. There was an audible gasp from the crowd of guests.

191

Danny glanced at Jason, who gazed at Nicole with eyes that looked slightly dazed.

Beside him Tom watched Nicole's stately approach with the expression of a deer caught in the headlights.

Bet that dress weighs twenty pounds, Danny thought irrelevantly as she gracefully moved past him. He could hear the faint clicking of the pearls that carpeted the train of her dress as she continued to move.

Along the aisle people smiled, oohing and aahing. Here and there Nicole turned her head and acknowledged their smiles.

The walk seemed to take forever. Danny fervently wished he were in a dream—one of those anxiety dreams where people walk and walk but never reach their destination.

Unfortunately this was no anxiety dream. This was an anxiety nightmare. And it was really happening.

Jason took Nicole's hand and watched her with the expression of a man who had just been confronted by a vision. Tom stood beside him, looking tall, stoic, and reassuring.

How did Tom have the nerve? How could he stand there right next to the man he had betrayed, smiling benignly at the woman with whom he had cheated? Danny felt his anger rise and struggled to keep calm.

The captain cleared his throat. There was an

expectant rustle from the guests. "Of all the honors associated with being the captain of a ship, perhaps the greatest honor of all is the authority to marry two people who are deeply in love. People like Nicole and Jason."

A derisive snort escaped Danny. The redhead next to him turned and gave him a curious look. Danny sank down a bit in his seat and glared at the wedding party.

Captain Avedon smiled at Nicole. "Marriage, like seafaring, is an old and honorable tradition. And marriage, like seafaring, attracts honorable people."

"Yeah, *right*," Danny muttered under his breath.

This time the look the redhead shot him was a rebuke. Danny sank even lower.

"Marriage is a long voyage. And not necessarily an easy one. Sometimes it's smooth sailing." He chuckled lightly at his own joke. "And sometimes it's very, very stormy." He gave the maid of honor and Tom an avuncular smile. "During those storms, the married couple depends on their trustworthy first mates to help them navigate the rough waters."

Another loud and derisive snort escaped Danny. This time it was loud enough to turn heads all the way up to the fifth row. The redhead next to him leaned close. "If you can't be quiet, leave," she hissed.

Danny saw Isabella turn in her seat. Her eyes met his and narrowed dangerously. The message was coming through loud and clear. "Shut up!"

Danny set his jaw and took a deep breath, determined not to snort anymore—no matter how much hypocrisy he witnessed.

"So without further ado," the captain said. "Let us proceed with the ceremony."

Isabella turned forward again. Danny's eyes bored a hole in the back of Tom's head as the captain repeated the familiar words of the marriage ceremony.

Danny stole a look at the faces around him. Every face wore the same fatuous look. The same silly gullible smile. Tom and Nicole were making fools of each and every well-wisher. They were making a mockery of one of the most sacred institutions in the world.

This was a farce. A Restoration comedy at sea. It was wicked. Evil. *It's unethical!*

"If anyone here knows of any reason why these two should not be joined in matrimony, let him speak now or forever—"

"Stop!" Danny shouted, jumping to his feet.

The crowd reacted as if a gun had been fired. Some people let out a shriek, some gasped, some groaned. The captain dropped his book.

Nicole, Jason, Tom, and the maid of honor whipped their heads around to see who had spoken.

A low buzz quickly escalated to an excited babble.

"Quiet!" the captain shouted. "Please, ladies and gentlemen. Be quiet."

Nicole's face was as white as her wedding dress. And Jason's face was a sort of green-gray.

"Did someone say something?" the captain inquired.

"*I* said something!" Danny fumed. "This couple cannot get married."

Danny noticed with a grim sense of vindication that Nicole clutched at Tom's arm for support rather than Jason's.

"Why on earth not?" Captain Avedon demanded.

"Because the bride has been two-timing the groom, that's why," Danny said.

One of the bridesmaids fainted dead away. Before she had even hit the floor, Jessica Wakefield shot up out of her seat. "Look who's talking," she shouted angrily.

Danny's eyes bulged in surprise. "What does that mean?"

Of all the irritating expressions she'd seen on men's faces, the "who, me?" look was the one that made Jessica the most furious. Mr. Danny Ethics Wyatt had the moral integrity of a flea. How dare he ruin a perfectly nice wedding when he was just as guilty of cheating as Tom and Nicole?

Jessica threw her clutch bag down on her chair and put her hands on her hips. "I saw you and Nina Harper kissing in the movie theater, you hypocrite."

"That's a lie!" Nina protested, jumping angrily to her feet.

Jessica watched Isabella's angry, glittering eyes focus on Danny. *You tell him, Isabella,* she thought.

Then suddenly, without warning, Isabella's dangerous gaze shifted to Jessica. "You knew Danny and Nina were fooling around and you didn't tell me?" she shouted incredulously. "Some friend *you* are. Jessica Wakefield, don't you ever speak to me again."

Isabella grabbed her purse, hurried out of her row, and ran sobbing toward the exit.

Jessica's jaw fell open and Danny looked as stunned as she felt.

But before she could say anything, two of the groomsmen broke into a loud argument, one of the bridesmaids began to hiccup loudly, and Nicole let out a loud and miserable wail. Then she charged down the aisle.

"Nicole! Wait!" Jason shouted. He started after her but could hardly make his way through the crowd. Pandemonium erupted.

It was as if the ship had hit an iceberg and everyone onboard had been thrown into a panic.

*　　　*　　　*

196

Danny stared toward the exit in horrified shock. It was as if he'd thrown a live grenade into the ballroom. He'd never seen so much confusion.

"Leave me alone!" he could hear Nicole's shrill and tearful voice shouting. "Leave me alone!"

Jason forged through the crowd and grabbed Danny by the lapels of his jacket. "Are you crazy, Wyatt? Are you trying to completely ruin my life?"

"I'm trying to save it," Danny protested.

"By making horrible accusations against Nicole?" He shook Danny as hard as he could. "Leave me alone! Stay out of my life from now on. Please!"

Danny had made no move to defend himself. And he wasn't going to. Even if Jason started swinging.

A smaller pair of hands grabbed Jason's and began furiously trying to detach them from Danny's lapels. "Stop it," Nicole shrieked. "Leave him alone."

But Jason was too angry. "You heard what he said about you," he said through gritted teeth. "He owes you an apology."

"No, he doesn't," Nicole choked out. She grabbed Jason's sleeves and yanked as hard as she could. "Because it's true."

Jason released Danny so abruptly, Danny almost fell backward. "What?" Jason whispered.

Nicole's lips trembled. "It's true. He did see me and Tom kissing, but . . . but . . ."

Jason stared at Nicole with a stunned face. "I thought you loved me," he said in a hurt and bewildered voice. "I thought you wanted to marry me. To spend the rest of your life with me."

Nicole's shoulders shook. "I'm sorry," she sobbed. "I thought I did, too." She grabbed the skirts of her heavy wedding dress and ran for the door.

"Where are you going?" Jason yelled.

"I've got to get away from here. I've got to get off this ship."

"Come back," Jason begged.

He took off running just as one of the waiters made a desperate attempt to retreat from the room with a tray of hors d'oeuvres.

Jason and the waiter collided. Danny watched the gleaming silver tray fly into the air, flip upside down, and rain a selection of round and squishy finger food all over the floor.

Jason's heel landed on one of the hors d'oeuvres and he went skidding across the ballroom floor as if on skates. "Nicole!" he shouted as he careened into a row of folding chairs with a loud crash. "Don't do anything crazy!"

As Danny watched his best friend disappear under a pile of collapsible chairs, he was suddenly overwhelmed with remorse. He'd never seen such genuine pain on anyone's face as he had just seen on Jason's and Nicole's.

"Nicole! No!" he heard someone outside the ballroom shout.

The shout was followed by a shrill scream of terror.

"She's going over the side," someone else yelled in a panicked voice.

Danny's heart gave a painful thump. In a million years, he'd never imagined things getting so out of control. He pictured Nicole balanced on the rail, ready to fling herself over the side.

In that twenty-pound dress, she'd sink like a stone.

And it'll be my fault, Danny realized. "Gangway!" he shouted, lowering his head like a bull and charging through the crowd.

If he had driven Nicole over the side, it was his duty to save her.

He heard grunts and groans around him as he cleared a path like a quarterback on a football field. Seconds later he was out on the deck, where there seemed to be hundreds of people.

"Nicole! Come back!" someone yelled over the rail.

"Leave me alone!" he heard Nicole shout from somewhere below.

He leaned over the side and his eyes widened. Nicole had climbed into one of the lifeboats and was lowering it into the water by means of a winch.

"Where are you going?" her maid of honor shouted.

"It doesn't matter," Nicole wept. "I can't stay here."

Two guys leaned over and grabbed the ropes, trying to pull the boat back up.

Nicole stood in the boat and yanked the ropes. "Let go," she screamed hysterically. "Let go!"

"Nicole!" Elizabeth shouted at her. "Sit down. You're rocking the—"

The entire deck screamed as Nicole tumbled out of the side of the boat into the water.

Chapter
Eighteen

Tom reached the deck rail just in time to see Danny disappear into the water. His heart pounded in his chest. All that seemed to be left of Nicole was a soggy veil floating on the surface.

Two orange life vests smacked the surface of the water.

But no one surfaced to grab them.

Tom was just pulling off his jacket when Danny broke the surface. A split second later he pulled up a sputtering and coughing Nicole.

Gasping for air, Danny reached for one of the life vests and helped Nicole get her arms through it.

The crowd on deck began to cheer wildly. Tom's face broke into a relieved grin. Suddenly a hand closed over his shoulder.

Tom turned just in time to see Jason's fist come sailing through the air straight toward his jaw. He heard the punch before he felt it. It wasn't a hard blow, but it caught him by surprise. The next thing Tom knew, he'd lost his balance and was falling.

The water was surprisingly warm and not altogether unpleasant. Once he kicked off his shoes, he felt pretty confident as a swimmer. *If one more person punches me,* he thought irritably, *I'm really going to start getting annoyed.*

Several yards away Nicole paddled around in the water. She was still refusing to return to the ship. Danny paddled after her, trying to convince her he was sorry and that he had never meant to cause so much trouble.

Tom looked up and saw what seemed like a hundred curious faces staring at him over the side. This scenario wasn't exactly what he and Todd had planned, but it was close.

"Help!" Tom cried, splashing around in the water. "Help." He flailed his arms a few times like a scared four-year-old. Then he let himself fall below the surface.

Fortunately he'd always had a large lung capacity. As a child, it had allowed him to stay underwater long enough to send every adult around the pool into a panic.

It had been a lot of fun when he was in the fourth grade.

It wasn't as much fun now. He could feel the seconds ticking by. Wasn't Elizabeth ever going to save him?

Just as he was about to give up and surface, a strong hand firmly cupped his chin. The next thing he knew, Danny was hoisting him up out of the water.

As soon as their heads broke the surface, Tom scowled. "Get lost."

Danny's brows rose. "Get lost?" he repeated in a surprised tone. "I just saved your life, and all I get in the way of thanks is 'get lost'?"

Tom nodded. "Get lost. Buzz off." He began to swim away, but Danny followed.

"Tom, please. I know we've been on the outs, but I'm sorry. I realize now how wrong I was to stick my nose in and—"

Tom turned in the water, smacked the surface with his palm, and set a spray right into Danny's eyes and nose.

"Hey!" Danny protested.

"Get away from me," Tom ordered, swimming off. As soon as he was several yards away he began swinging his arms again. "Help!" he cried. "Help me. I can't swim."

Todd looked frantically around. Where was Elizabeth? Tom couldn't keep up that act forever. It was only a matter of time before someone else jumped in to save him.

Down in the water, Nicole bobbed around in her orange life vest. Her wedding dress billowed around her, making her look like a vestal jellyfish.

Another figure went diving over the rail, hit the water, and then dog-paddled toward the other life vest. It was Jason. "Nicole, honey. We have to talk."

Todd's eyes scanned the crowd, but he didn't see Elizabeth. Then a familiar voice penetrated the din.

"Nina! Isabella! Be reasonable."

Todd ran for the ballroom. Sure enough, there was Elizabeth. As always, she was determined to be peacemaker.

Nina and Isabella faced each other, their arms crossed in front of their chests.

"There's nothing going on between me and Danny," Nina protested.

"It seems to me there's something going on between you and *everybody*!" Isabella countered.

Elizabeth held up her hands. "Stop it. Both of you. You're acting like children. If you would just sit down and—"

Todd never gave her the chance to finish her sentence. He reached out, grabbed her upper arm, and began dragging her out on the deck.

"Todd!" she sputtered in an outraged tone. "What are you doing? Let me go! I'm talking to . . ."

Todd used his free arm to elbow his way through the crowd toward the rail. "Look!" he said, pointing to Tom.

Down in the water, Tom flailed around. "Help!"

Elizabeth's eyes opened wide in surprise. She screamed as Todd lifted her in his arms and heaved her over the railing.

"Have you lost your . . . miiiiiinnnnnnnd!" Elizabeth screamed as she fell toward the water.

A million thoughts raced through her mind at once. *I'm never speaking to Todd Wilkins again,* she vowed to herself, landing in the ocean water.

She briefly fell beneath the surface. Elizabeth kicked off her shoes, scissored her legs, and resurfaced with no trouble at all. She rubbed the salt water from her eyes and looked around. Not two feet away, Tom dog-paddled beside her. "Help!" he said in a very unworried tone.

"Excuse me," Elizabeth said. "Did you say something?"

"I asked for help," Tom replied.

"Give me one good reason why I should help you."

"Because you love me more than you'll ever admit."

"Ha!" Elizabeth said, swimming away and back toward the boat.

Tom swam after her. "Danny's got things all wrong. Yes, I did kiss Nicole. But she's not interested in me, and I'm not interested in her. I'm interested in you. I'm in love with you."

Elizabeth kept swimming.

"Help!" Tom said behind her, easily swimming after her.

"Stop that."

"Help me, please," he cried dramatically.

"Cut it out. Get Nicole to save you. Or your new best buddy, Jason."

"It's not the same," he complained. "I want you to save me. If you love me, you'll save me before I drown."

"I don't love you," she insisted. "And I don't care if you drown or not."

"Oh, really?" Tom asked pleasantly.

"Really," Elizabeth confirmed.

"Well . . . bye, then." He fluttered his fingers in farewell, then slipped out of sight.

"Man, this is wild," Gin-Yung said. "In fact, this is the most exciting thing that's happened for days."

"Has anybody ever told you that you have a morbid sense of entertainment?" Noah asked dryly.

Gin-Yung nodded. "Yep!" she said, looking happily around her as people ran in nine different directions and various bells and alarms began to ring.

Deep in the crowd, Noah saw Alex being buffeted by the surging people. All at once a rush of uncontrollable anger swept over him. Where was Leonardo? If he was so crazy about her, why wasn't he making sure that she was protected from the crowd?

His eyes narrowed when they found Leonardo on the other side of the deck, trying to forge his way through the crush of people.

"Excuse me," he said to Gin-Yung.

Noah took off at a run, shouldering his way through the crowd until he was standing behind Leonardo. He tapped him on the shoulder, and Leonardo turned and gave him that cordial but slightly supercilious smile that Noah had come to despise.

"Yes?" he asked. "What can I do for you?"

Noah pointed toward the sky. "Look up there for a minute, will you?"

Leonardo's gaze automatically shifted in the direction of Noah's pointing finger, and as he lifted his chin, Noah brought his right fist up and delivered a knockout uppercut.

Bruce arrived just in time to see Leonardo collapse on the deck. "Darn," he muttered at Noah's elbow.

Noah jumped guiltily.

"I was just coming over here to punch him myself."

Noah drew himself up with as much dignity as he could. "I didn't *punch* him. He, uh . . . *fell.* . . ."

Bruce grinned. If that was the way Noah wanted to play it, that was fine with him. But if it had been he who'd decked the guy, Bruce would have had it emblazoned on a sweatshirt. "Sure, Noah," he said. "You're right. He fell. I saw him fall." *Right into your fist,* he thought, trying hard not to laugh.

"Leonardo!" a female voice gasped.

Bruce saw Noah give another guilty jump as Alex appeared. She knelt beside Leonardo and felt his pulse. "What happened?" she demanded, looking up at Noah and Bruce.

"He fell," they explained in unison.

Tom counted off the seconds, wondering at what point Elizabeth would start to panic. He pictured her treading water above him, waiting for him to come bobbing up to the surface.

Right about now, she'd start to wonder where he was. She'd look around, thinking maybe he'd swum away under the water. But she wouldn't see him.

He grinned and let out a few bubbles for effect.

This was the point at which one of his parents had usually panicked and dived in after him.

Moments later he felt a hand cup firmly under his chin.

By the time he broke the water, his lungs were screaming for air. "You *do* love me," he gasped.

"I do not," a deep voice argued.

Tom shook the water out of his face and scowled. "Danny! I told you to get lost."

He heard a giggle behind him. When he turned, he saw Elizabeth laughing at him. She sent a spray of water in his direction with her hand, which Tom took as a challenge.

Laughing himself, he took off after her.

Alex held Leonardo's hands between hers and waited for Noah to return with a cup of water. A little smiled played around her mouth.

Leonardo hadn't fallen. Noah had punched him. Alex had seen it with her own eyes—which was the only reason she could believe it. She would never have believed that Noah would do anything so . . . well . . . *passionate* unless she had witnessed it firsthand.

She didn't approve of violence, but at least she knew now that Noah wasn't completely indifferent to her. In fact, he must be pretty crazy in love with her to do something so completely out of character.

Nina appeared beside her and gasped. "Oh, wow! What happened?"

Alex met her gaze squarely. "He fell," she said evenly.

Bruce pounded on the cabin door with his fist. "Lila! Let me in."

He'd seen her hurry down the stairway to her cabin.

"Go away," she cried.

"Let me in, or I'll knock the door down."

"Go away," she repeated, obviously in tears.

"I'm serious," he warned. He backed up all the way down the hall. He'd never actually knocked a door down before. But he'd seen it done in the movies a million times. How hard could it be?

He was up to speed by the time he was halfway down the hall. And as the door loomed larger, he threw himself into the air and angled his shoulder—just as the door swung open.

"Look out!" he screamed as he went flying into the room, careened across the cabin, and knocked all of Lila's perfume and makeup bottles off the dresser. He sprawled on the floor.

"Bruce!" Lila hurried to his side and bent over him with large and anxious eyes.

He reached up, grabbed her, and pulled her down on top of him. He pressed his lips against hers and put every ounce of his heart into a searing kiss.

She struggled at first, but then melted in his embrace. "Oh, Bruce," she whispered. "I love you, and I don't know what to do."

He rolled over, jumped to his feet, and pulled her up. He put his hands on her shoulders and looked her in the eye. "Lila. Listen to me. Okay? Tisiano is dead. We're alive. And while we're here, we have a duty to enjoy the time we have on this planet. Now, I happen to know that the Calypso Spa, one of the greatest resorts in the

Caribbean, is less than fifteen miles away."

He took her hand and began pulling her out of the cabin. "What we're going to do is grab one of the lifeboats, get off this loon boat, and have a real vacation."

"But what about Leonardo?" she cried. "Where is he?"

"Don't worry. He's being taken care of."

Chapter Nineteen

Jessica hung over the rail, watching Elizabeth and Tom. They were treading water and kissing.

"Bombs away!" she heard a group of boys shout. They vaulted over the side and splashed down into the water.

Laughing and shrieking, several girls kicked off their heels and followed suit.

The wedding had turned into a pool party. And once again, Jessica was without a date.

The boat sprang to life with a ferocious roar. "All right!" Bryan said happily. He grabbed the skis and threw them in the water. "Let's start from here and not stop until we get there. If this motor dies, I might not be able to get it started again."

Old Pierre nodded and moved toward the wheel of the boat.

Bryan lowered himself into the ocean, put the skis on his feet, and grabbed the rope.

"Ready?"

"I'm ready," Bryan answered.

The boat gave another roar and dragged Bryan up out of the water. Seconds later he was skimming toward the huge white cruise ship, just the way he had in his dream.

"So there's nothing going on between you and Danny?" Isabella asked Nina. "You're sure?"

Nina grinned. "Isabella. I think Danny's one of the all-time greatest guys in the world. But he's not interested in me. And I'm not interested in him."

"Then who *are* you interested in?" Isabella asked impatiently as another group of kids jumped over the rail and splashed down in their party clothes.

A movement on the water caught Nina's attention. She looked out at the water and did a double take. "Bryan?" she whispered.

"Faster!" Bryan shouted to old Pierre. "Faster."

Pierre nodded and gunned the engine. The boat's speed practically doubled. Bryan felt as if he were skimming along on an air pocket inches above the water.

He felt great. Supremely confident. He almost

wished there *were* a big orange incline in the water.

There was *something* in the water up ahead, though. What was it? It looked like a series of . . . He squinted. What? Buoys?

Old Pierre saw them too. He seemed to realize what they were a split second sooner than Bryan did. Just as it was sinking into Bryan's head that those dark round things bobbing in the water were human heads, Pierre jerked the wheel of the boat and pulled a U-turn in order not to accidentally run over any swimmers.

The ski rope went slack and then taut like the tail of a whip. When it snapped, Bryan went flying, tumbling head over skis through the air in what he felt sure was the most spectacular wipeout in the history of the Caribbean.

"Bryan!" Nina shrieked. She kicked off her shoes and without a word to Isabella dove over the rail. She began swimming the minute she hit the water, using the racing stroke she had worked so hard to perfect when she was a teenager.

Bryan was insane. What had possessed a man who couldn't swim to go skiing in the ocean with no life vest? And that fall had probably left him unconscious.

Her strong arms sliced through the water and her head turned like a piston with each stroke. Her rhythmic swimmer's breathing technique helped her to stay calm and focused. After swimming several yards, she lifted her head out of the water for a moment to get her bearings and see how far away his body was. But then her eyes widened.

Bryan wasn't floating facedown in the water. He was *swimming*. The well-formed muscles in his arms stood out in high relief. He gracefully moved through the water in her direction.

"Bryan!" she choked, feeling as if her heart were about to burst. She threw her arms around him as soon as he was within reach. He let out an alarmed cry as their combined weight pulled them beneath the water. Immediately she released him and they both came up for air.

"I'm still a beginner," he said apologetically as he dog-paddled beside her. "I'm afraid I can't float and hug at the same time."

"That's okay," she said softly, leaning forward and kissing whatever part of his bobbing facial anatomy she could reach. "I think you've made a great beginning."

"Why didn't you tell me swimming was so much fun?" he asked a few moments later as they made their way toward the cruise ship.

Tom reluctantly withdrew his lips from Elizabeth's. "As much as I hate to break this up, I probably owe Jason and Nicole an apology."

"I'll come with you," Elizabeth offered.

Tom and Elizabeth swam through the crowd of kids in the water until they found Nicole and Jason holding hands and earnestly talking while they floated in their orange life vests.

"Jason," Tom said. "I want to apologize to both of you. I'm sorry about what happened, and I'm sorry this wedding is such a shambles."

Jason looked dour for a moment, but then his face relented. "And I'm sorry I hit you. Listen, Nicole and I have been talking. It's pretty obvious to both of us that we're not ready to get married."

"It's not that we don't love each other," Nicole said to Elizabeth. "But I think both of us sort of freaked out when we realized how incredibly permanent marriage really is."

"So I guess things really worked out for the best," Jason said.

Elizabeth shook her head, laughing. It looked as if everything was going to be okay after all.

Then she looked up and saw a very dejected-looking Jessica staring out over the festive scene.

Jessica gripped the rail until her knuckles were white. *Who are you? Who are you?* Where was her guardian angel? Didn't he have any idea how lonely and left out she felt?

She desperately wanted someone to share things with. Someone besides Elizabeth. Practically everybody on the cruise was in the water now—and they were all having the time of their life.

A brilliant thought occurred to her. So far, her guardian angel had made appearances only when she was in some sort of danger. Obviously the best way to conjure him was to pretend to be in distress.

She placed her purse carefully on a deck chair and removed her shoes. "Help! Help!" she cried just before she threw herself over the rail.

"Do I have to jump in to convince you that I care?" said a voice at Gin-Yung's elbow.

Gin-Yung jumped in surprise and stared up at Todd's handsome face.

"No," she said. "But let's go in anyway." She lifted both her small hands and shoved against his chest with all her might. He tumbled backward, disappeared under the water, then came up laughing.

Gin-Yung kicked off her penny loafers and dove in after him.

"Isabella, I'm so sorry. If it's any consolation to you, I've learned my lesson. And you know there's nothing between me and Nina, don't you? What Jessica saw, she misinterpreted."

"Don't touch me!" Isabella warned as Danny approached slowly, dripping and sloshing.

"But I'm sorry," Danny said. "I'm really, really sorry." He lifted his arms and rivulets of water poured off folds of his shirt.

217

Isabella backed away.

"Can't you forgive me for being such a jerk?" he begged, reaching toward her. His feet left wet footprints along the deck.

She lifted her hands and motioned him back.

"I've learned my lesson. I'll never jump to conclusions, make judgments, or stick my nose in anybody else's business again."

"*Please* stay away from me," she begged.

"Isabella!" he wailed. "I can't go on like this. Tell me you forgive me."

"I forgive you," she said quickly, still backing away.

"Tell me we're back together," he pleaded.

"We're back together," she blurted.

"Tell me that you love me," he urged.

"I love you," she agreed in a high voice.

He reached for her, but she let out a loud shriek. "Don't touch me!"

"Why *not*?"

"This dress is *rayon*!"

"Help! Help!" Jessica cried.

But there was so much shouting, she could hardly hear her own voice. Maybe she needed to get a little farther out, where she could be seen as well as heard. She swam confidently through the warm ocean water until she was slightly apart from the crowd around the boat. "Help! Help!" she tried again.

But no strong arm wrapped around her waist.

She bobbed around and did her best to look distressed. But no one appeared to rescue her. After five minutes, she decided it was useless.

Jessica flopped over on her back. Might as well rest a little while before swimming back to the boat. The sun felt warm on her face, and soon she was so relaxed, she felt as if she could almost fall asleep.

"Jessica! Help," she heard a voice say a few feet away.

She blinked open her eyes. Good grief. She really had fallen asleep. And she'd dreamed somebody had called for help.

"Jessica!" the voice said again. "I really need your help."

This time she knew she wasn't dreaming. She immediately came out of her floating posture and looked around. Several yards away, she saw a handsome face in the water. He smiled, but the face was white around the lips. "I've got a cramp," he said.

Even though he was in the water, and Jessica couldn't see exactly how tall or broad he was, she knew instantly that the guy calling for help was her guardian angel. She could read his love for her in his eyes.

Jessica began swimming over to him. "Don't worry," she gasped, so flustered she could hardly think. "I'll get you back to the boat."

He lay on his back and Jessica put her arm around him. She stroked hard with one hand and propelled them both through the water toward the boat with scissor kicks.

As soon as they reached the side of the boat, Jessica helped him grab the side of one of the several lifeboats that now dotted the water. Ship's personnel sat in the boats, pulling people out.

The PA system began announcing that there was the possibility of sharks, and even the most intrepid of the swimmers began moving back toward the ship.

Two strong men pulled her mystery man up out of the water. Again, Jessica was astonished at how tall he was. As soon as he was settled in the boat the sailors extended their hands to help her in. But Jessica was in too big a hurry to be ladylike. She ignored their outstretched arms, put one leg over the side of the boat, and scrambled up. She couldn't wait another second for a good at her mystery man.

"Ooommph," she cried as she tumbled into the boat. She raked her hair out of her eyes and looked around.

"Hello, Jessica," he said in a deep voice. An amused smile lurked at the edge of his lips.

All of a sudden, the surface of the water seemed to shift and she had a sensation of whirling vertigo. It was as if her life were a tape rewinding before her very eyes—all the way back to grammar school. She opened and closed her mouth a few times, unable to speak or even breath. "Oh, my God!" she finally managed to squeak. *"It's Randy Mason!"*

Leonardo's eyes opened. Alex and Noah sat back on their heels, relieved. "Leonardo," she whispered. "How do you feel?"

Slowly he sat up and looked around. "I feel very strange," he said. "Where is everybody?"

"In the ocean," she answered.

He nodded and began to stand. "Leonardo," Alex said as she helped him to his feet. "I have to talk to you."

Leonardo looked at Alex's face.

"Is it about your career?"

"No. It's about—" Alex broke off, clearly unsure of how to continue. Noah protectively took her hand and squeezed it. He waited, with his heart in his throat, until he felt the answering squeeze.

The gesture spoke volumes. "She wants to talk to you about us," he said confidently, finally certain that his deep feelings for Alex were returned.

Leonardo stared at them in bewilderment. Then, as understanding slowly dawned, his face fell slightly. He reached out and sadly stroked Alex's cheek. "I think I know what you want to say. It's written on your face. And his."

"I'm so sorry," she choked out.

"Me too." Leonardo sighed. "I'm losing a wonderful girl and a supermodel at the same time. But . . ." He stared at them for a long, long while. Then he nodded as if he were resigned to accepting something he had struggled against. "What can we do?" he asked wearily. "We love the ones we love. We cannot always make our hearts do what we would like them to do."

Noah cleared his throat. "That's very astute," he said.

Leonardo walked over to the rail and looked at all the activity below him. "So much happiness," he murmured to himself.

He appeared to think for a long time. Finally he spoke. "Life is very short, isn't it? Shorter for some than for others."

For the first time, Noah felt sorry for Leonardo. He'd lost his brother, and it was obvious that he missed him. Now he'd lost Alex too. Noah knew from firsthand experience how hard that could be.

"So if life is so short, it makes no sense to turn away from happiness." Leonardo hung his head. "I think I caused a lot of problems by coming here. A lot of pain. For you. And for Lila. Do you think she truly loves Bruce?"

"I think she does," Alex said softly.

"And Bruce? Does he truly love her? Will he make her happy and treat her well?"

"I think so," Noah answered.

"Then they must be together," he said decisively. Leonardo gave them both a wide smile. "One must be gracious in defeat as well as victory," he said, giving Noah's hand a hearty shake. "There is a resort on the next island. Tonight you will all be my guests for dinner and dancing. Will you please extend the invitation to the others while I go lie down for a while? I seem to have a headache." He reached back and gingerly felt the back of his skull. "By the way, what, exactly, happened to me?"

"You fell," Alex and Noah said together.

Chapter
Twenty

"Lila!" Bruce knocked on the door. "Are you ready?"

The door opened and Lila stood, radiant, in a beautiful new evening dress purchased from an expensive shop in the Calypso Spa. "Oh, Bruce. Coming here was the best idea you ever had. I've had a bath, a massage, a manicure, and a pedicure. I feel like a new woman."

He put his arms around her and pulled her to his chest. "I knew if we could just get away from that ship and everybody on it, we'd have a fighting chance at happiness. Come on," he said. "There's a five-star restaurant awaiting us. And I'm starved."

"Me too," Lila said. "This is the first time I've had an appetite in days."

Arm in arm, they strolled down the elegant hallway of the Calypso Spa. The soft light of the seashell-shaped lamps created a rosy glow on the delicately tinted tropical wallpaper.

"I love my friends," Lila said dryly. "But being around them and all their problems is just so . . . incredibly stressful."

"Ditto," Bruce agreed as they entered the lobby and passed the lounge area. "I could very happily spend the rest of spring break with you and only you. I wouldn't mind staying here for the rest of the semester. I've got a pocket full of credit cards, and if I never saw a familiar face again, it would be—"

"Bruce! Lila! Yoo-hoo!"

Lila let out a little shriek, and Bruce rocked back on his heels. "Winston! Denise! What are you guys doing here?"

Winston and Denise hurried toward them, wearing fancy shorts and shirt outfits and big white bandages on their heads. Winston grinned broadly and Denise hugged Lila. "We washed up on the beach opposite the golf course. Then we both got conked on the head with flying golf balls," she explained.

"We spent all afternoon in the infirmary. Management's been real nice about everything. They gave us clothes, rooms, and food." Winston laughed. "I think they're afraid we're going to sue."

Bruce took Lila's arm and began to pull her away. "It's like some strange kind of nightmare," he said softly. "Maybe if we just ignore them, they'll disappear and we'll be alone again. Come on, let's—"

"Lila! Bruce! We wondered where you were."

Bruce whirled again and groaned.

They were pouring through the front door like an invading army. As he watched in horror, everyone he knew walked into the Calypso Spa. Elizabeth Wakefield, Tom Watts, Jessica Wakefield with some good-looking tall guy, Isabella Ricci, Danny Wyatt, Todd Wilkins, Gin-Yung Suh, Noah Pearson, Alexandra Rollins, Nina Harper, Bryan Nelson, Jason Pierce, Nicole Riley, and bringing up the rear—*Leonardo*.

Virtually every single person from whom they had hoped to escape was now assembled outside the main dining room.

Bruce squared his shoulders and scowled as Leonardo's eyes met his. Then he rolled up his sleeves, prepared to do battle if the guy had enough nerve to try to forcibly drag Lila out of the spa.

Leonardo hurried toward them. But when he stood face to face with Bruce, he didn't lift his fist. He opened his arms, grinned, and kissed Bruce's cheek with a loud smack.

"I can't believe it," Jessica breathed, lacing her fingers through Randy's as they waited for the four-tiered dessert cart to visit their table.

The group had just dined on the outdoor patio at large tables with beautiful centerpieces. A live band played soft music in the background, and now that dinner was over the laughing, raucous group had subdivided into whispering romantic couples.

"I can't believe we're actually sitting here together. Why wait so long? Why all the mystery?" she asked.

Randy smiled, and Jessica felt a thrill of electricity just looking at his gorgeous face. He looked as if he'd stepped right off a movie screen. "Jessica, my family moved away from Sweet Valley after the sixth grade. I've remembered you all these years—I don't think I ever stopped having a crush on you. Then I saw you on campus, and I couldn't believe it. You were even more gorgeous and vivacious than you were in middle school."

Jessica blushed happily. "So? All you had to do was tap me on the shoulder and . . ."

". . . and say what? Hi! Remember me? Randy Mason, the school nerd."

Jessica giggled.

"If I'd done that, what would you have remembered about me?"

"Well," Jessica hedged. "I might have remembered the way you always had peanut butter stuck in your hair."

"And masking tape on my glasses."

"And a leaky pen in your shirt pocket."

"And geeky pants that were always an inch too short."

"And—"

Randy cut her off by raising his hand. "Enough. I think I've made my point."

"So you thought you had to do something really special to convince me you weren't a nerd anymore?"

"You got it!"

"I'd say saving my life five times is really special. That's some metamorphosis! You're like Heathcliff. You go away a nerd. You come back as my tall, dark, and handsome guardian angel."

"So did my plan work?" he asked, squeezing her hand slightly.

By way of an answer, Jessica leaned forward and kissed him softly.

"Alone at last!" Tom said, folding Elizabeth in his arms and feeling hers twine around his neck. They were dancing in a secluded corner, low and sexy music in the background.

Elizabeth giggled. "I'll bet that's exactly what Bruce was saying to Lila when we all stampeded in. I never saw anybody look so bummed out to see his friends."

Tom laughed. "I know how he felt. And by the way, I'm going to say a prayer tonight thanking whoever was responsible for sending Jessica's guardian angel."

Elizabeth giggled again. "It's nice to know she won't be popping up every twenty minutes."

Tom leaned down and kissed her ear. "There are a lot of guys here tonight. But I think I'm the luckiest one."

Elizabeth looked up and smiled wickedly. "You know what?"

"What?"

"I think you are too."

Elizabeth laid her head on Tom's shoulder, closed her eyes, and prepared to enjoy what was left of their six-day, seven-night vacation. It was going to be the best spring break of their lives after all.

Elizabeth is more in love with Tom than ever. But when a dangerously powerful man decides he wants to make Elizabeth his partner for eternity, she may not be able to resist him. Find out what happens when Elizabeth encounters the dark side, in the next Sweet Valley University Thriller Edition, **KISS OF THE VAMPIRE.**

SIGN UP FOR THE
SWEET VALLEY HIGH®
FAN CLUB!

Hey, girls! Get all the gossip on Sweet Valley High's® most popular teenagers when you join our fantastic Fan Club! As a member, you'll get all of this really cool stuff:

- Membership Card with your own personal Fan Club ID number
- A Sweet Valley High® Secret Treasure Box
- Sweet Valley High® Stationery
- Official Fan Club Pencil (for secret note writing!)
- Three Bookmarks
- A "Members Only" Door Hanger
- Two Skeins of J. & P. Coats® Embroidery Floss with flower barrette instruction leaflet
- Two editions of *The Oracle* newsletter
- Plus exclusive Sweet Valley High® product offers, special savings, contests, and much more!

Be the first to find out what Jessica & Elizabeth Wakefield are up to by joining the Sweet Valley High® Fan Club for the one-year membership fee of only $6.25 each for U.S. residents, $8.25 for Canadian residents (U.S. currency). Includes shipping & handling.

Send a check or money order (do not send cash) made payable to "Sweet Valley High® Fan Club" along with this form to:

SWEET VALLEY HIGH® FAN CLUB, BOX 3919-B, SCHAUMBURG, IL 60168-3919

NAME _____

(Please print clearly)

ADDRESS _____

CITY _____ STATE _____ ZIP _____

(Required)

AGE _____ BIRTHDAY _____ / _____ / _____

Offer good while supplies last. Allow 6-8 weeks after check clearance for delivery. Addresses without ZIP codes cannot be honored. Offer good in USA & Canada only. Void where prohibited by law.
©1993 by Francine Pascal   LCI-1383-123

Life after high school gets even *Sweeter!*

Jessica and Elizabeth are now freshmen at Sweet Valley University, where the motto is: Welcome to college — welcome to freedom!

Don't miss any of the books in this fabulous new series.

Your friends at Sweet Valley
High have had their world
turned upside down!

Meet one person with a power
so evil, so dangerous, that it
could destroy the entire world
of Sweet Valley!

A Night to Remember, the book that starts it all, is followed
by a six book series filled with romance, drama and suspense.

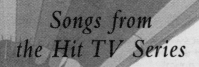

Songs from
the Hit TV Series

Featuring:

"Rose Colored
Glasses"

"Lotion"

"Sweet Valley High
Theme"

Available on CD and Cassette
Wherever Music is Sold.